HeartsBlood
BOOK THREE
Deathless

Previously published as Ripe, Wild Strawberry by Lena Fox

Published by Fairies and Fantasy Pty Ltd 2021
ISBN: 978-1-922390-33-2 (paperback)
ISBN: 978-1-922390-34-9 (hardcover)
Deathless (Heartsblood Book 3) copyright © 2018 Selina Fenech.
All rights reserved. www.selinafenech.com
Formatting design © 2021 www.kiladesigns.com.au

SELINA A. FENECH WRITING AS

LENA FOX

1

OWEN

I could only stare at Kaitlyn as the jet engines roared in my ears, merging with the sound of my racing heartbeat.

A million images flashed through my head. A million possibilities. A million feelings.

Kaitlyn's pregnant.

One horrible possibility hit me so hard it knocked the breath from my body. My mind spun back to the nightmare we just lived through—the Scarl trying to rape the woman I loved, *my Strawberry.*

I couldn't breathe through that thought, couldn't speak around it.

Kaitlyn whispered, "Owen, say something."

Her fingers reached for mine and I felt her trembling, shivering like a bird caught in a trap.

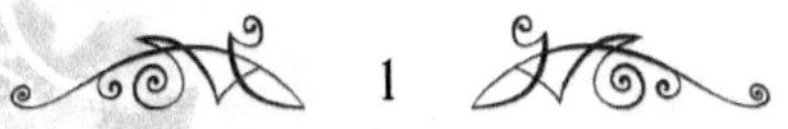

I gulped in thin air and muttered, "The Scarl. He … is it …?"

"No." She shot out that single, terse word. Her fingers clamped down tightly on mine. A red flush rushed up her neck and over her cheeks, and her eyes blazed. "He never … It's ours, Owen, from the night after we escaped. It's yours."

Mine. I was knocked speechless all over again. I'd never considered being a father.

Vampires didn't reproduce. Couldn't reproduce. Not counting siring, which is entirely different. It had never occurred to me that I'd have a *child.* Kaitlyn was always the one having to remind me about protection and contraception since I became human again. And that night after we escaped the Starved, so desperate for the comfort of each other's touch, we had both forgotten.

And now … there was a new life growing inside Kaitlyn. Life we'd created. I couldn't even grasp that monumental concept. Being human again was still so new to me, I hadn't yet spent time considering creating *more* humans. Whether it was something I wanted. Whether it was something I deserved to do.

I looked past Kaitlyn to the window behind her, blacked out for the non-humans on board. I glanced over my shoulder, seeing no one, but knowing we weren't really alone. The Ebonguard assigned to us were nearby, making themselves unseen and

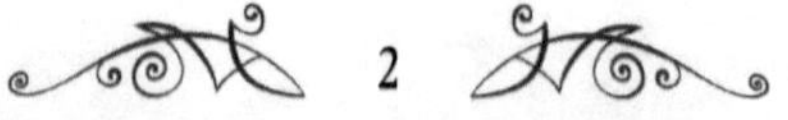

unobtrusive, but there, watching, listening. I scowled. Our invisible bodyguards were eavesdropping on our private conversation. But this was *happening. Now.*

Taking slow breaths, I tried to process the immensity of it. I tried to calm myself. But I couldn't shake the memory of Kaitlyn on that sacrificial altar. It slammed into my head like a steel mallet. What if she was wrong? If she was lying, or had blocked out the trauma? What if the child growing within her wasn't mine, or human at all, but the offspring of a dark ritual?

My heart rocked back and forth in my chest. I wanted to kill the monster who assaulted her. I wanted to fight, to scream. But the enemy was dead already, and right now, it was just Kaitlyn, staring at me with eyes full of vulnerability, fire, and hope, waiting for me to respond.

The longer I said nothing, the more I saw her eyes grow dull.

Say something. "This is …" I didn't know what this was. My body was processing too many emotions to know up from down. A small ball of happiness and excitement had sparked deep within me, but its warmth was smothered beneath too many doubts. I wanted to tell her it was good, it was wonderful, but our lives were still too complicated for good or wonderful to exist in.

Everything shifted and stretched outward into a future I had never thought to want, and wasn't

sure Kaitlyn wanted either. She'd said she wasn't ready for children. Her contraceptive implant the Scarl removed was meant to last for *years*. She'd just earned her big acting break. She'd finally gotten the career she'd always dreamed of. Was there any room in there for a baby?

Was there any room in her life now for me, after what had happened to us? Had it tainted our relationship too darkly? I swallowed back the anger that swelled within me. Anger I could barely contain. I was still relearning my own human life, these overwhelming emotions. How could *I* raise a brand-new human?

As if she'd been reading my mind, she said, "It's still really early, only days. Normally too soon to know for sure, but what with my weird situation, and all the tests … Still, it's not too late for the pill."

How could birth-control pills work now? She was already pregnant. Not that I understood much about modern contraception. "Not too late? I'm sorry. I'm not following you."

Kaitlyn's throat worked, visibly swallowing. She pulled her hands free of mine and they went to her blouse, smoothing away imaginary wrinkles in the emerald green fabric. "I mean I can get an abortion pill."

"Abortion?" The word roared from my mouth before I even thought through what she'd said. My blood grew hot as my emotions firmed themselves

in my mind. *I could be a father. I want to be a father. I want this child.* "No."

"I know it sounds harsh, but we have to think about this logically." Her face contorted, eyes shimmering with unshed tears. She drew a long breath. "Beyond normal human worries about being ready for this, we have that prophecy dogging us, vampires who may or may not be our enemies, and … I have a whole lot of mixed feelings. I don't know if I want to terminate this pregnancy. I just know I have to consider it. We both do."

I heard all her words but the one that buzzed the loudest in my brain was terminate. It was so final. "I will not consider that."

A hard, vertical slash appeared between her brows. "Because you were *so excited* about having a child a few moments ago. Either we want this, or we don't."

I gaped. Was she right? Did I only want this now because of the threat of it being taken away? Maybe we should be thinking about all our options. Maybe the fact I wasn't instantly excited by the idea meant I wasn't ready. But the news had shocked all logical thought from me, and my head still reeled from it, unable to lock down a solid thought or emotion, except one. "You can't do *that* to my child."

Her eyebrows tilted upward. "*Your* child? It's *my* body, and the *child* is barely a tiny cluster of cells right now." She shifted away from me in her chair, folding her arms. "I should have known you'd be this way! Ugh, you're so ... I'm going up against the mindset of a person who's over four hundred years old. You vampires may have sorted out some of your sexist ways, but you're still way behind on dealing with who owns a woman's reproductive organs!"

This was going so far off the rails. I didn't understand what she wanted; I didn't understand the scope or consequences of our options. I was only starting to feel what I wanted.

I took a long, slow breath, and asked the question I should have from the start. "Do you want this?"

Kaitlyn's mouth froze in an open position, and then trembled. The light of hope, vulnerability, and something deeper and indistinguishable shone in her eyes again. The slightest turn of a smile formed on her lips as she began to speak.

Before she could, she was interrupted by the flight attendant approaching with a rattling food cart. A clean, crisp white cloth covered it nearly to the floor, and she stopped it just in front of my seat. "Let me arrange the table for you."

Her short blond hair was tidy and pinned back, but she still brushed it with her hand, almost nervously. I wondered how much of our conversation she'd managed to hear. I almost sent her away again. But an interruption was good to let my thoughts catch

up. Kaitlyn pursed her lips and gave a small shrug.

We hadn't ordered anything, so I assumed this was a parting gift arranged by Lance. The flight attendant deftly spread china plates and then silverware onto our small table. She reached to a lower shelf of her trolley and revealed a platter of fresh fruit, cheeses, delicate crisps of toasted bread, and thinly sliced, very rare beef. Then she brought up a slender bottle the same color as Kaitlyn's blouse. I shuffled about in the seat, uncomfortable in the silence, my gaze going back to Kaitlyn. I wanted the flight attendant to go away, but I also didn't want to keep fighting. The attendant being there was simply staving off the inevitable, but I took it because I needed a moment. I needed more than a moment.

The attendant set two small, ruby-red aperitif glasses on the table. The green bottle chinked softly against one glass and the sound, the sight of that bottle and those particular glasses, caught my attention. The flight attendant continued placing things on the table, and I was struck by the oddness that this same flight attendant from our previous flight was with us again.

A sense of something worrying grew inside me. Something *wrong*. But what? I knew there were puzzle pieces right in front of me, but I couldn't put them together. My gaze went from the bottle, to the glasses, to the silver tongs sitting in a small bowl filled with

delicate little cubes of sugar. But I was still bogged down by my argument with Kaitlyn. Still trying to absorb the concept that Kaitlyn was pregnant. I couldn't seem to grasp the current situation or what was wrong with it.

What am I missing?

In a soft and strained voice, Kaitlyn said, "None for me, thank you. Not a fan of absinthe."

Absinthe?

Was this Lance trying to be funny?

The wormwood in it burns vampires, and I might not be a vampire anymore, but I was still getting used to being human, and not particularly willing to drink things that may or may not be deadly to me.

The flight attendant poured one glass, straining the absinthe over a sugar cube. "And you, sir?" she asked, in a voice that should have sounded perfectly polite and correct but had a rim of tension running below it.

I was going to refuse but she'd already lifted the aperitif glass toward me. It glowed like a jewel, filled to the rim, and a waft of the herbal, anise scent reached my nose. Then her hand turned, just slightly. Not by much. A mere eighth of a rotation of her wrist. If I hadn't been staring at the glass so intently, I would never have noticed that slight spin. How intentional it looked.

The glass tilted. The liquid hovered in the air.

Everything felt like it had stuttered down into slow motion. The green drops fell, then landed with a splash on the back of my hand.

I caught my breath, held it for a moment, but only felt the coolness of the alcohol evaporating off my skin.

The flight attendant seemed to hold her breath too.

Kaitlyn grabbed one of the folded linen napkins from the table and dabbed at my hand, and where a few drops of absinthe tinted the white shirt at my wrist. She seemed concerned only by staining, oblivious to anything else.

The flight attendant acted flustered, but eyed me carefully. "I'm so sorry. Are you all right, sir?"

I bolted up out of my seat, snatching for the flight attendant's collar. She shifted quickly, keeping her high-buttoned shirt and neatly tied neck-scarf out of my reach. Her eyes narrowed.

Kaitlyn gasped. "Owen! It was just a spill!"

I yelled out into the cabin, "Ebonguard!"

Two vampires in all black appeared as though from thin air. Kaitlyn squeaked in surprise. Even though I knew what to expect, I was still shocked at how well their compulsion powers had hidden them from our human eyes.

"Grab her," I commanded the Ebonguard. I knew one was Joss. The other was Val. At the moment they were impossible to distinguish.

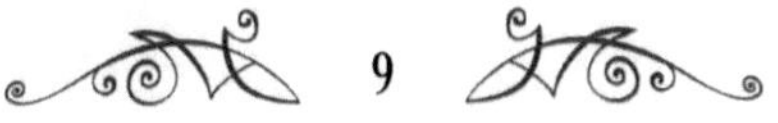

One of them lunged for the attendant. She tried to dodge, but wasn't fast enough, managing only to bash up against the trolley as she was caught.

"What's going on?" Kaitlyn got to her feet.

The Ebonguard held the attendant tight around the shoulders as I reached over and yanked her neck-scarf off and pulled open the top of her shirt.

Right below her collarbone was a green-black mark of a knife surrounded by a ring of fire. A tattoo I knew too well.

My suspicions were confirmed. She was one of Alam's Blades. The absinthe spill had been a test.

Kaitlyn stammered, "Who … what … Owen!"

"Vampire hunter."

"*What*?" Kaitlyn seemed more insulted than any-thing. "But we're not vampires!" she yelled at the Blade.

But the attendant must have known I was a vampire once. How long had she been tracking me? And she'd followed me to Umbravallis, discovered I was now human … That was all dangerous information for the followers of Alam to have. She couldn't be allowed to escape.

The Ebonguard must have realized this as well. The one holding her shifted quickly as though to snap the woman's neck.

With her cover blown, the flight attendant didn't hold back. Blades were still human, but she moved with almost inhuman speed and flexibility. She slipped through the Ebonguard's neck-crushing fingers. Something clicked inside her sleeve, shooting a slim canister into her hand. She twisted it and a cloud of mist burst into the cabin.

I couldn't avoid getting a mouthful of the gas, and quickly identified the unique, rotting scent. Nemexia.

I shot the Ebonguard a fearful look. If the corpse-flower knocked them out, Kaitlyn and I would have no chance of stopping the Blade.

The Ebonguard swayed, unsteady. They each grasped at their fabric head-coverings, and pulled an additional layer of fine, filtering material across their already covered faces. They stumbled but stayed upright.

The Blade scowled, her pretty face twisted with ruthless anger. She reached beneath the covered food trolley. When her hands came back into view, they held a chunky black weapon the size of a sawn-off shotgun. It hummed to life like a camera flash recharging.

My arms swept out for Kaitlyn, trying to get her behind my body, to somewhere safe.

Both Ebonguard rushed the Blade, but they were slowed by the Nemexia, moving at a more human speed.

The Blade took aim. A streak of brilliant blue laser-sharp light shot from the end of the gun.

One Ebonguard jumped to the side. The other took the full brunt of the burst.

The Ebonguard loosed a high-pitched, female scream. The blast burned straight through her clothing, scorching away the fabric across her shoulder, taking most of the shoulder with it. Flakes of grayed skin peeled away.

Waves of false sunlight radiated through the cabin. The Ebonguard's scorched flesh smoldered then caught, flames and light exploding through the vampire's body.

Then she was gone, leaving only ashes drifting through the air.

"Joss!" Kaitlyn screamed.

"I'm here," the remaining Ebonguard called back.

Kaitlyn clutched me tight, and I felt the same relief. And the same fear as the gun hummed again. Joss was good—for now—but the other Ebonguard had been no match for that sunlight weapon. *What the hell is that thing?* It had been a long time since I'd encountered a Blade. Their tech had clearly advanced.

Joss was moving faster again, still not at her normal speed, but enough to get herself behind the woman. She planted a high kick into her back and sent her flying a few feet across the space. The Blade crashed into the wall. She was on her feet again in seconds.

Deathless

My arms remained around Kaitlyn, desperate to protect her. What would Alam's Blades do if they found out about Umbravallis? About a vampire becoming human again? About the unborn child at the center of a vampire prophecy? I had to help Joss stop this woman from escaping.

I shoved Kaitlyn down behind a seat. "Stay here," I panted, then I ran, hands up and balled into fists.

My knuckles crashed into the Blade's jaw just as she was preparing to fire another blast from her weapon. The beam missed Joss by a hairsbreadth and shot a hole straight through the cockpit door.

The plane shifted, tilted. Then went into a violent spin.

I grabbed onto a seat and was pressed into it by centrifugal force. I couldn't get to Kaitlyn, who was clinging to a seat as well. She screamed. Her body twisted and spun, her hair flying up from her head.

Through the hole into the cockpit, I made out the pilots spraying fire extinguishers onto their control panel.

The plane banked again, and we went tumbling around like toys thrown carelessly from a child's hand. I lost track of the Blade, and Joss, as tablecloths and fruit smashed into the wall beside me. The plane whipped us right to left. Gray filled my vision. Ashes in the air. *Val.* I tasted her ashes in my mouth, breathed them into my nose and throat, unable to

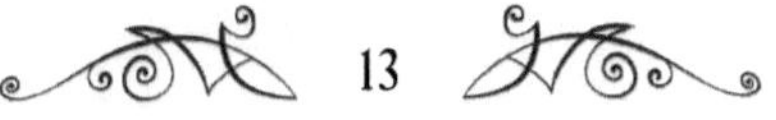

do a damn thing about it. My head struck the edge of an overhead locker.

I couldn't see Kaitlyn anymore. I screamed her name just as the plane finally, mercifully, leveled out then flew straight and true for a few precious seconds.

Joss and Kaitlyn re-appeared from behind a pair of seats, Kaitlyn with a cut cheek, blood dripping off her jaw. She gave Joss a nod of appreciation, then Joss scanned the cabin.

The Blade was down the other end, strapping something to her back. A parachute? She leveled her weapon again, but it wasn't aimed at any of us. She pointed it straight at the wall of the cabin.

No, we'll all die!

I ran toward the vampire hunter.

I'm too slow.

The gun went off. The blowback lifted me off my feet. I crashed into the opposite wall. An enormous hole had opened in the side of the plane and the Blade went out of it.

Wind tore through the cabin, sucking everything toward the hole and the sure death that lay beyond. Kaitlyn screamed. Her hands were wrapped around a seat, but the explosive decompression had snapped it off its base. Her and the seat flew out the gaping hole.

"Kaitlyn!" My scream was lost in the whip of the wind and the sound of the plane tearing itself apart.

Deathless

The last thing I saw of her was one of her hands wrapped desperately around the side of the hole, then even those fingers were gone.

She can't be ... can't be gone.

The suction from the initial burst eased, but I ran toward the hole, as though I was flying out of it as well.

I was snatched back by Joss. "Stop. The pilots are regaining control of the plane. They can make a safe landing."

"Kaitlin can't!" I snarled, fighting her grasp.

I lunged again for the hole. The sun was just setting and clouds swirled by, and Kaitlyn was *out there.* Falling. Every second took her closer to the ground. She had, what? Maybe sixty seconds of freefall before she needed to open a chute? A chute she didn't have. I had been counting the seconds since she disappeared. *Nine, ten ...*

Joss threw me back across the cabin. I moved to fight her again then blinked, noticing that she'd strapped her tactical backpack onto her chest and a parachute on her back.

"I only have one chute. I have to take out the Blade. She's my priority. She's a threat to Umbravallis. But ... I'll see what I can do for Kaitlyn." Without waiting for a reply, she launched herself out the hole as fast as a bullet.

That wasn't good enough. *Fourteen, fifteen ...*

Joss thought I'd stay in the cabin. She was dead wrong. The only thing I knew for sure was I had to get to Kaitlyn. The woman I loved was falling, and there was no way I wasn't going after her.

I moved to the edge of the hole. The rushing wind blurred my vision, but I could just make out the three falling bodies below me. The Blade, in flight attendant white and gray. Joss all in black. Kaitlyn, in green. *Kaitlyn.*

I had to get to her. Fast, and before it was too late. *Seventeen, eighteen.*

I jumped, aiming my body for the woman I loved with no other plan than to be with her.

If she died, I died.

2

KAITLYN

I'm outside the airplane. I'M OUTSIDE THE AIRPLANE. It was every bad dream I'd ever had. It was a nightmare come to life. I could hardly believe it was reality, despite the sparkle of sunset in my eyes and the air roaring past me and the cold whipping through my clothes. I was falling, and I couldn't stop.

Maybe I didn't want to stop.

Falling wasn't the lethal part. The landing—that was what would kill me.

I stopped screaming, only because I couldn't draw in enough breath. My heart seemed to have expanded to five times its normal size, pummeling my insides, pushing all the air from my lungs.

Breathe. Think. My ability to reason had taken just as large a leap as my body had. I tried to focus.

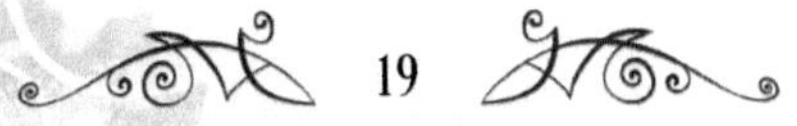

I tumbled toward Earth. *How fast am I falling? How long do I have until I hit the ground?* I had no idea how high the plane was before I got sucked out of it. The little part of my brain that was still alert, and trying to think of a plan, insisted that the plane had to have dropped quite a lot, because if it hadn't, I'd already be dead. If I'd fallen from our cruising altitude, I'd be dead, frozen, or suffocated, or something, right?

Yeah, okay. So the plane had dropped a lot. That just meant the ground was coming at me sooner rather than later. I wanted to brace for that. Or should I stay loose and flexible and roll with it, so I could absorb the impact? Hadn't that worked for someone, once? I couldn't remember what was real, what was a one-in-a-million chance I could cling to, and what was foolish hope. I just wanted to think of a plan to help me stay alive.

And to help that tiny spark of future life inside me stay alive too.

I wanted it. Despite everything, despite logic telling me to consider all options, I wanted to have this child.

I found enough breath to scream again, a scream born of sheer rage at the injustice of it all. My hands clawed at empty air in the hope of finding some kind of handhold, some kind of braking system I knew didn't exist.

I couldn't tell which way was up, and I spun

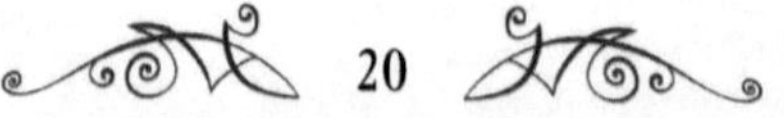

uncontrollably, my hair catching in my mouth and eyes. I had to level out, stretch out, catch the air like a gliding squirrel. I giggle-sobbed hysterically. *As if that will save me.* I didn't know how long I'd been out there, *outside the plane*, seconds that felt like forever.

I stretched out my arms and legs, star-like. I flipped again, wobbled, then steadied horizontally on my back, staring up at the darkening sky above me. *Better than looking down, I guess.*

Shadows, blurry against the dusky sky, hurtled down after me.

They zoomed closer, taking shape. Two lean figures, rocketing headfirst, streamlined and fast. One headed off to my right, all black. The other came straight for me. I saw a white shirt, dark hair. *Owen? Joss? No.* Sorrow swept into me, threatening to upend whatever was left of my mind. They must have been sucked out of the plane too.

Joss shifted angles suddenly, heading to Owen. She was bulkier than usual, and she caught Owen quickly. They flew together for bare seconds, while she strapped something to Owen. Hope burned unbearably in my chest, along with confusion and grief. They hadn't fallen. They'd jumped. That was a chute she just strapped to Owen. But if she'd had the chute, did that mean she'd needed one and now didn't have one?

Joss grabbed Owen, spun him around in an orbit of her body, building speed, then threw him straight at me. His body shot toward mine, faster than before. The air wobbled me and I almost flipped into a spin again. I had to stay level, so Owen could reach me in time to open the parachute and save us both. If we still had enough time. I didn't dare look down to see. I could barely stand the intense fire of hope and fear waging war inside me.

A beam of light zigzagged across the sky, and I turned my head. The flight attendant. No, the vampire hunter, Owen had called her. Right before everything went crazy. She had her weapon out, firing up at Joss who had changed direction to go after her.

Joss crashed into the hunter, sending them both into a spin, a hurricane of limbs and ripping fabric and beams of light.

The hunter's chute flew out, catching the air, and it seemed as though they froze in place while I dropped out from beneath them with frightening speed.

A body slammed into me, grabbed me tight, and we tumbled together. Ropes and red fabric zipped and whizzed free, and a sharp jerk jolted my neck painfully.

Our tumble stopped. The ripping wind stopped. The fall became gentle.

Owen's body was as familiar as my own. He had caught me, and he shouted at me to hold on. *No kidding.* I held onto him tighter than I knew I could, and he returned that embrace.

"I've got you," he said.

Deathless

The hunter's heavy gun swished through the air beside us, and I craned my neck to try to see Joss. They were above us, slightly to the right, still a brawling mess. The hunter's parachute was ripped, and Joss tore it completely free, off them both. She tried to reach for the ropes—too slow. It fluttered away above us all, like a blood-stained kite. Joss kicked the clawing hunter off her. The hunter screamed. Joss and the hunter fell fast, one after the other, too far away for Owen and me to do anything to help. The hunter's cry curdled in my chest. She'd caused all this, she'd tried to kill us all, but I knew the very same fear just moments ago that she was feeling now. And nobody, nothing, could save her. Tears stung my windburned eyes.

And Joss … could she survive this? I had no idea.

The ground was so close. Dusk hid most of the earth, but I could make out the tops of trees that would either break our fall or break every one of our bones. Or be hundreds of potential wooden stakes for a vampire traveling at terminal velocity. This wasn't going to be a smooth landing, even with a chute. Horror stretched its arms up and enfolded me in its cold embrace.

The hunter hit the tree line first. Her screaming stopped. She disappeared without even a thump.

Joss hit next. She smashed through the forest like a meteor, thundering and cracking trees in her

path. *Joss … don't die.*

Then it was our turn.

"Hold on, just hold on!" Owen yelled.

I wanted to laugh at him being Captain Obvious again but holding on was all I could do as leaves brushed our feet.

Branches snagged and grabbed at our clothes. We pinballed from trunk to trunk. The ground rose fast, and we crashed down. We skidded out of each other's embrace. A rock slammed my hip and dirt flew up into my nose and mouth. I tumbled to a grazing stop. Owen fell beside me, and the shredded red silk of the parachute collapsed over us.

I waited a full ten seconds, counting, breathing, too scared to see if my body was in one piece, if I had really survived. Owen turned his eyes to mine; blue, alert, and swimming with relief.

Tears ran down my cheeks, salty and warm. I wiped them with my hands and saw that some of the warm wetness was blood, and could have been from my torn palms or my stinging face.

Warily, testing our bodies, we pushed away the remains of the parachute and got to our feet. We were battered, torn, but we could stand.

We were alive.

Owen dragged me immediately into his embrace. I pressed my mouth to his.

My high-pitched laughter of relief escaped between

our lips, and I looked up at Owen. "You saved me. You are, completely sincerely, my fucking superhero."

He was also out of his mind. But I kept that to myself. He'd jumped from the plane, after me, and he hadn't even had a parachute until Joss gave him hers. He jumped—and he did it to save me. And it could have all easily ended far worse than it did. My knees went weak, and I staggered closer into his body.

We held each other for a long moment, and I enjoyed each precious breath.

I whispered the worry on my mind. "Do you think Joss made it?"

"I did."

I jumped right out of Owen's arms and my own skin. "Damn it, ninja-woman!" I clutched my chest and turned around to see Joss. She stood behind us, leaning heavily against the thick trunk of a pine tree. Her backpack was resting at her feet.

She was wrecked. The loose silk layer of her ninja-like Ebonguard uniform had been torn almost completely off her, but there was another layer underneath, something high-tech and skin-tight, like a bullet-proof thermal. The metal armor that normally protected her neck and top of her chest was gone—who knew how or where or when. Her cowl was lost as well. Luckily the sun had completely dropped, so barely any light remained under the canopy of evergreens around us. Joss's party-pink hair glowed against her dark skin and dead-serious expression. Her face was a mess of cuts and scratches that didn't bleed, her hair tangled full of pine needles. One cheek had a black singe mark straight from jaw to hairline.

In her left shoulder, terrifyingly close to where her heart might be, a branch the size of a police baton was impaled right through her.

I pushed my wobbling legs over to stand beside her. Owen followed me.

My eyes filled again with tears.

Joss noticed. "The Nemexia is still slowing me down, slowing my healing, but I'll be fine." She looked down at the branch. "Could do with some help getting this out though."

The blood drained from my face and I probably turned green. But I nodded.

Joss turned around to face a tree, gripping it with her arms. Owen and I grabbed onto the stick protruding from her back.

"On three," Joss said.

"Oh god," I said.

"One, two …"

Joss pressed her shoulder forward into the tree trunk, pushing the stick through from the front as Owen and I pulled. The stick slowly, stickily, slid free.

I squealed the entire time. Joss didn't make a sound.

We dropped the stick on the ground.

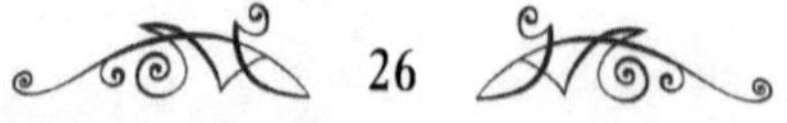

"Are you, do you need—?"

"Have you seen the Blade?" Joss went straight to digging through her pack. She pulled a black scarf out and wrapped it around her head and face, leaving only her eyes visible.

"Blade?" I asked.

"The vampire hunter," Owen explained. "They are called Alam's Blades."

"They are *theys*?" Not just one vampire hunter, but a group of them? It might have been good to know there were vampire hunters out in the world, if *they* considered Owen and me included in their list of enemies.

Owen told Joss, "We saw her hit the trees, not even sure which direction anymore. Haven't seen her since."

"You yanked off her chute. She has to be dead. Right?" I said.

"Here." Joss pulled some bundles from her bag and threw them near our feet. "I have to go confirm the kill, clear up her remains. I can't let her, or anything she may have recorded, make it back. Not with the information she could have."

"Y-you're leaving us?"

She zipped up the rest of her kit, put it on, and strode away, disappearing quickly into the growing gloom without another word.

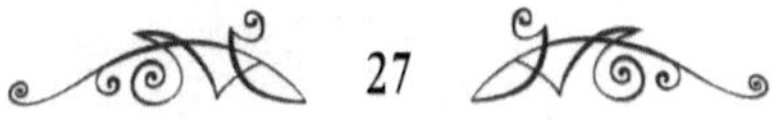

3

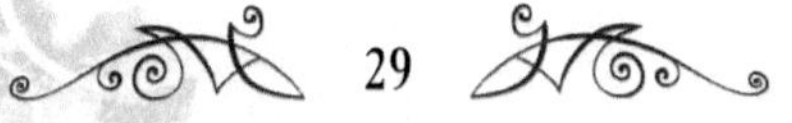

KAITLYN

I stared around at the woods, fright sending long shivers through my body. The temperature had plummeted and we were out in the middle of the mountains of Who-Knew-Whereania.

Owen knelt down, going over the bundles Joss had left behind. He picked up and clicked on a torch. The light should have made me feel better, but it only made us seem smaller, a tiny glow in an endless black forest.

"It's okay," Owen comforted me. "Joss has us covered. Look. There's a tent."

"How nice. Is there a hotel room in there? Maybe an espresso machine? Some chocolate or a bag of chips?"

He straightened and shone the torch at me.

I held my hands up. "Don't you dare judge me

right now. We almost died. AGAIN. I want a bed, a soft one, and all the comfort food in the world. You know I'm a nervous eater."

Owen chuckled. "I know. I'm sorry, but I don't think a hotel is in the kit. Or an espresso machine. There is ..." He picked up a silver-wrapped package and squinted at it, "some sort of dehydrated stew."

I grouched out, "Yum. What is Joss even doing with that stuff? She can't eat it."

"She's looking after humans. She's got to have human-care supplies, I suppose."

"Sure. Obviously she was prepared for the event of a crazy flight attendant vampire hunter blowing a hole in our plane and stranding us in the middle of the wilderness." I was so upset that I actually kicked a rock. And because everything wasn't screwed up enough already, I also happened to be wearing darling little open toe sandals. "Ow."

"Did that make you feel better?"

"Yes." I pouted. My petulant voice cracked and tears started flowing again.

Owen gathered all the bundles of gear into his arms and stood up. "Kaitlyn, we can survive this. We can survive anything when we're together. I need you now."

My breakdown halted in its tracks. I was still shaking all over from the massive dose of adrenaline and the temperature that was dropping as fast as I just had. I managed to find a breath and take it. He needed me. I needed him. We were out here in the woods, and we needed to survive, together.

"Okay. Okay, I'm good. What do we do now?"

"Find some water, and somewhere to set up this tent and build a fire. It's getting cold fast, and there's not much else to do in the dark until Joss or someone else comes for us."

I limped over to where he stood and gathered up the smaller supplies as he pointed the torch for me.

Owen tilted his head, quiet for a moment. "I think I hear running water. Might be a stream that way."

I followed his lead, and it only took a few minutes of careful stumbling through the forest to reach an open, grassy area leading down to a slow-running, rocky creek. Owen shone the light around, and it looked almost pretty. Lush green grass with flowerheads, closed for the night, bobbing softly above. The stream giggled and burbled as the water made its way around the weather-smooth stones. I would have loved to have picnicked there in different circumstances.

The trees stood back from the stream, giving us a window to a sky of brilliantly bright stars, and allowing the half-moon to cast its glow on our campsite.

Owen stomped an area of grass flat, and we put all our supplies down and took stock. A compact emergency tent. A thin, plasticky, two-person survival sleeping bag. A small first-aid kit. An empty canteen and water-purification tablets. The bag of dehydrated stew, a metal bowl, and a spork. It was already chillingly cold, so we gathered small branches from the edges of the clearing. Owen stacked them on a large flat outcrop of rock, in the shape of a neat nest, with a bundle of fine dry fiber in the middle. Just one strike of the waterproof matches from the kit and we had a nice little campfire going.

"Ooh." I stared at the warm licks of flame. "Girl like man who make fire."

Owen chuckled. "Some of my old skills from being a soldier way back when are still with me."

By the firelight, we washed our hands and faces in the stream, and applied some basic first-aid to our cuts and grazes. We filled the empty metal flask with water, put a purifying tablet in and gave it a good shake, then left it to sit to do its thing. We were lucky everything was labelled and had instructions. Owen had the tent—a low dome barely wide enough for two—popped up in just moments. All we had to do to make the stew was pour water into an opening in the bag, reseal it, and lay it near the fire to warm up. We sat there, waiting for our dinner, watching the flames leap high and golden.

Owen poured some of the stew, which smelled and looked just as appetizing as dehydrated and then rehydrated stew sounds, into the bowl. He gave it a stir, then lifted a sporkful to my mouth.

It tasted almost like real food, except for that weird aftertaste that all highly processed and packaged-for-long-shelf-life foods have. The pieces of meat, small and few, had a spongy consistency.

I managed to swallow it. "Too bad that cheese from the plane didn't fall out with me."

Owen's pale blue eyes twinkled as he spooned a bit of the slimy concoction into his mouth. "Surely you could have pocketed some while you were being sucked out of the aircraft."

I smiled back at him and we shared the stew, mouthful by mouthful, snuggling close together. Between the fire, the hot food, and Owen's body, I finally warmed up enough to stop shaking.

Hoots and growls and cracking noises came from the woods, and I scooted even closer to Owen. His living heat seeped into my skin, reassuring me. An unwanted image of him as an ice-cold vampire came to me, and I shivered. *He is my real, human, living Owen,* I told myself. *He'll never be that monster again.*

He cleared his throat softly. "I'm sorry I reacted so badly before, about the pregnancy. I just … I never imagined I'd be a father. It took me by surprise, and I couldn't sort through my feelings fast enough."

"I'm sorry I sprung it on you like that. I guess I was hoping you'd know what to do and say, because I'm honestly terrified."

Owen squeezed me softly. "It can't be worse than what we've already faced, right?"

The flames leapt and danced, painting shadows on his handsome face, and my heart hurt so much I looked down to make sure I hadn't gotten a tree branch to the chest like Joss. Tears started up, and I couldn't stop them. "That's just the thing. We've faced so much. Too much. We've been kidnapped, tortured, fed on, enthralled, chained up, and starved nearly to death in that horrifying cavern. Dragged into dark rituals and creepy prophecies, had our fates decided by an inhuman court. Oh, and then we were attacked by a vampire hunter and sucked out of a plane. We've seen so many horrors, and I feel like we're far from guaranteed we won't be tormented with even more. I don't know how to deal with all of this. I don't. And adding a baby to the mix?" My voice faltered and my hands shook.

Owen tossed a piece of wood onto the fire. The flames made a roaring, sucking sound. His voice was rough with emotion. "I thought I'd lost you when you were sucked out of the plane."

"Yup. Well, if I wasn't suffering PTSD from everything already, tonight probably tipped me over the edge there. I am for sure seeing a shrink when we get home."

Owen started to talk, but I wasn't done. A rant had come upon me and I had to let it out. "As if it wasn't enough to be worried about vampires wanting my super-tasty blood, or to treat me as a science experiment or prophecy mommy, now I have to worry about vampire hunters too? I mean, you're not even a vampire anymore. I was never a vampire! We're, at the most, vampire adjacent. Like, in the same neighborhood but we don't invite them over for barbeques."

His chest moved. A rumble of laughter came from his mouth.

I elbowed him. "It's not funny."

His hands wrapped around mine, warming my fingers. "I know. You have to trust me, Kaitlyn. I will always protect you."

I wanted to believe him. And I did believe he'd always try—he'd jumped out of a damn plane to save me. But he couldn't promise he'd always succeed. I reached over and gently touched his chest. I felt so protective of him. I wanted to always save him too, but how could I? I felt so weak, so powerless, so useless against what was out there.

I didn't know how I could keep myself and Owen safe from everything threatening us. How could I protect a defenseless child? Even now, so early along, I felt a desperate, fiery yearning to keep that tiny life safe. *I will keep us all safe. Somehow.*

As though on the same mental page, Owen said, "I'll protect both of you." And he put his hand on my tummy.

My breath caught, and my eyes stung with tears. The forest seemed to hold its breath for a moment as well, silent around us.

I blurted out, "I know we've just been through a lot and emotions are high and we should, really, think about this all properly while it's still early. And it's still so, so early that things can easily go wrong naturally, but ..."

"You want to have a child," Owen finished my thought for me.

"Mm-hmm."

"With me."

"Uh-huh."

"And be a family together for as long as our ever-after lasts?"

"Yeah."

Owen wrapped his arms around me, pulling me right up into his lap. "Me too."

Our arms went around each other, tears ran down our faces, and smiles spread on our lips. His two words had filled me with relief greater than I'd felt from landing alive after our fall. Love filled me even more.

A wave of pure desire rushed through me. A yearning, clinging, revelry of this love and life and *Owen*. My mouth met his. He returned my kiss with the same desperate passion and our tongues met too. For breathless moments, that was all I needed: the crush of our lips against each other, consuming each other, warming us more than our fire ever could. And then I needed more.

Owen lifted me from his lap, across onto the grass. I lay back into it, the feather-soft blades brushing up around my neck, crinkling under the thin silk of my shirt. My vision was haloed by a fringe of green as Owen bent over me, his mouth pressing against my neck.

Once upon a time that would have filled me with horror. But he was my Owen now. His touch sent shockwaves of longing through my system, crashing down all my doubts and fears.

His hands caressed my body, and mine relieved him of his shirt then moved down to his pants. Owen carefully removed my clothes, and the grass prickled softly under my bare skin, teasing and tickling. I pushed his pants all the way down and he kicked them off.

Our bodies met again, moving slowly together. His hands tangled into my hair, and he lifted my mouth to his in a kiss so deep that I couldn't breathe through it.

Our love was as slow-burning and intense as the stars that shone down upon us. Primal and deep as the woods around us. Hot and wild as the fire beside us. His every move sent me closer and closer to an edge I wanted to topple over. But I clung on, fiercely, to him and our pleasure and every beautiful moment we had, until ecstasy exploded through me. It felt like sparks flew from my body and my head filled with blinding light.

We curled up around each other. The fire roared beside us, touching our naked bodies with its heat, and we lay together in the glow of it and our love. For the moment, all I felt was grateful that we were alive, that we were together.

We drifted away to sleep in that little bubble of happiness. Just the two of us, and the baby who hadn't yet come to be. And I knew, beyond anything else, that I needed to find a way to protect us all. From any threat to our lives and our happiness. Nothing was more important.

I will do whatever it takes to make sure Owen and our baby are safe.

The rest of it, my career and the films I might have to say no to because of the pregnancy—that didn't matter as much anymore.

Our very lives felt so tenuous and fragile in the face of unknown horrors. How could I keep pursuing my dream of acting when our lives were still at risk?

There would be time for that dream to be dreamed.

After these nightmares were defeated for good.

4

OWEN

Light penetrated the thin walls of our tent, awakening me. We had shuffled in there during the night as the fire died down and we grew cold. The space-blanket sleeping bag crinkled as I propped myself up on my elbows, yawning.

Kaitlyn murmured something and rolled over. The plasticky cover was pulled taut over her body, outlining every curve. She was so beautiful it took my breath away. Long, wavy black hair, and a face like those carved into statues of angels and long fallen goddesses. The slim curve of her pale neck awoke a deep, dark hunger, stoking its way into life inside of me.

My bloodlust had been replaced by simple lust, human lust, but sometimes it felt too similar. I had

to look away. Kaitlyn needed more rest, and I needed space to think. I slipped out of the sleeping bag and stood up out of the tent.

A pearly light spread across the sky and treetops. When I was a vampire I'd lived for this moment—that time right before dawn when it looked like morning had come but it hadn't truly. The sun had not yet broken the horizon, but still spread a sheer wash of light over the sky that could be seen by eyes that couldn't handle true sunlight.

It was a moment that had anchored me to my forgotten humanity. To brave that light and force myself to remember had felt like strength.

Now I was human, and it felt like nothing but weakness. Sunlight and a stake to the heart were real dangers back in my vampire days, but now *everything* was a danger.

My scraped knuckles from the fall ached again as if to prove that point. As a vampire these trivial cuts would have already healed. I wouldn't even have had to think about whether I might get an infection that could kill me. Those things were serious now.

My eyes stung, and my body ached. I was dehydrated, hungry, and exhausted from stress and a night of rough sleep. That was the human condition, these pains and needs. I felt frail and very aware that I aged more every day.

I hadn't chosen this. Kaitlyn's blood had changed

me before I knew what was happening. I wondered, sometimes, if I'd have chosen this outcome otherwise. Now it was upon me, and came hand in hand with the gift of Kaitlyn's love, I accepted it. I treasured it.

But with all we'd faced, and could still face, could I continue to value Kaitlyn's love above her very life? Above the life of our child she grew inside her? Because as a human, I was powerless.

It wouldn't be hard to take back my vampire form. I had friends in Umbravallis who would take this mortality from me and return me to their kind. I remembered the pain of the change, of dying and being reborn in undeath. I would do it all to keep Kaitlyn safe.

But if I turned again, could I keep her safe from me? That blood of hers was intoxicating. Once I turned, I couldn't guarantee I would be able to control my thirst. I couldn't say I would treat her as more than just food, that I wouldn't enslave her again, for her own safety and the preservation of my delicious food source. Would keeping her alive be worth that?

I asked myself those questions like I'd already made up my mind to be bitten again. That was the only way I could be strong enough to save her, but it might also be the thing that got Kaitlyn killed. The only thing I knew for sure was it would mean sacrificing our love. I knew Kaitlyn only loved the human me, and I would be killing him.

My thoughts had fragmented into warring camps when I saw a familiar figure coming into the clearing. It was Joss, moving at top speed, trying to outrun the dawn. The sky grew pink and the tops of the trees wore a slim haze of gold, chasing her.

Without even a greeting, Joss went past me and flicked the tent flap open.

Kaitlyn groaned. "Turn out the lights."

I chuckled. Joss didn't. Turning out the lights was exactly what she needed. She ducked inside the tent, dumped her pack, and began digging through it.

Kaitlyn sat up. Her face had a crease on the right cheek and her eyes held a sleepy look but they cleared quickly. "Joss!"

Joss nodded and yanked on a coat and hood made of shimmery, thin material, specially treated to repel sunlight.

"Cutting it close?" I said.

Joss flicked a shady look at me. "Had lots to do. Decisions to be made." She pulled out protective goggles and put them on, then stepped back out of the small tent. Every part of her skin was now covered, but I felt anxious for her anyway. A vampire out in broad daylight was like a human stepping out into the vacuum of space—one chink in the protective suit could have dire consequences.

Some device in her pack made a static sound and

beep. She checked it, then threw a protein bar to each of us. "Time to move. Refill your water; it's a long hike to the pick-up spot. You can eat on the hoof."

"Pick-up spot?" Kaitlyn sounded hopeful, yet guarded. She scooted deeper under the sleeping bag cover. "Sure, just give me a moment to *get dressed*."

Kaitlyn leveled a look at me and I peered down at my own body. *And I'm standing here naked.* I retreated into the tent, and Kaitlyn and I dressed quickly. Joss covered the remains of our fire with dirt, then cleared up every sign of our campsite while we refilled and purified another canteen of water. Kaitlyn put her dainty sandals on with a pointed sigh. I gave her my socks to wear with them, but it was nowhere close to the hiking boots she'd need. I could tell my patent leather shoes were going to give me blisters in no time.

Joss adjusted her suit and the sun goggles. They darkened as the sun got higher in the sky, black like a welding mask. I knew they rendered her almost blind, but you could barely tell. Ebonguard were trained for conditions like this, trained to rely on their other senses so they were almost as effective without their vision as they were with it. She took the lead, moving us at a brisk pace.

We went into the thick reach of the trees. The sunlight fell in dapples, coin-shaped bits of light that moved and wavered and broke apart into patterns that looked like a glowing path. Kaitlyn moved straight through that spill of light, seemingly without even a moment's thought, because she had never had to think about it.

She caught up to Joss, and asked in a small voice, "What happened to the flight attendant?"

"The Blade's dead. I confirmed it. But we need to get clear of here because there's no telling how much intel got sent or who might be coming."

The sun weapon—that was some serious technology, and it was worrying what else the hunter might have had. I shook my head angrily. "She could have live-streamed the whole thing to anywhere in the world." *Shit.* I thought back to what info she may have gotten. "She deliberately checked to see if I was a vampire. She poured that absinthe on me on purpose to see if it would burn me. Either she suspected I was a vampire and was looking for proof, or she knew I had been a vampire, and was trying to work out if I was really human again ..."

That was the more worrying option. If that test was caught on video and sent out, if Blades knew I had changed, I was going to become their target. They'd want me to study me, and through studying and interrogating me they would find Kaitlyn. I was the weakest link. As an untrained human, I wasn't any match for the Blades. My hands clenched into fists, as though to spite my weaknesses. What else could I do? I already knew I would be getting Tiamat's ring back in my possession the first chance I got. That would be something. But I doubted it would be enough.

"Maybe you'll be lucky. She might not have even known you were a vampire in the past, and this was a simple hunt, confirm, and kill job, no recording necessary," Joss mused. She looked like some futuristic alien, and even under her protective covering she seemed itchy from the sun and pained by it. Every movement she made was tense. "But if they heard, somehow, that you were cured and they know now that you are, you have a massive problem."

Kaitlyn's lips had grown thin. "What are you saying?"

Joss hesitated. "I'm sorry. I have no clue whether the Blade got intel out of the plane. Her pack was … gone. I searched for hours in all directions, but there's not a trace of it to check what tech she had, to check delivery of data. Without being able to confirm nothing was sent, we have to assume the worst. We have to assume you and Owen are targets of the Blades. Which means you will be returned to Umbravallis."

Kaitlyn inhaled loudly through her nose. "You have got to be fucking kidding me."

Joss didn't reply. I knew Joss wasn't kidding. It made perfect, horrible sense.

"How many of these Blades are out there? Are they really such a big issue?" Kaitlyn huffed.

"The Blades of Alam have hunted vampires for almost as long as there have been vampires. Alam was one of the original seven. After they turned, he found he didn't much care for the violence and thirst that overtook him and the other originals. He decided they made a mistake, that they had no right to even exist. He left and trained humans to hunt his kin." I glanced around, paranoid at the very thought of the hunters. "Tiamat, the first original to die was at the hands of his hunters. It has been war ever since, and the cult of hunters grew only stronger and more devout after Alam's death. Hunters live only to destroy vampires; even their children are trained from birth to hunt and kill."

Kaitlyn's hands went to her belly, and I regretted mentioning children. She had to be thinking of ours and the dangers the child would face. It was exactly what I was thinking too. I took her hand, trying to offer some comfort.

Kaitlyn said, "And having a cure for vampirism, that would be another way to destroy vampires, wouldn't it? If they could weaponize it, force it on as many vamps as they could. It's exactly what the Synedrion was worried about. They won't ever let us go now, will they?"

I wondered for a guilty moment if the Blades

having the cure would be so terrible. The end of vampires, the end of immortality and bloodlust, could be a good thing, but I had a lingering sense of loyalty to the culture I'd been part of for so long. And to be captured by the Blades would only be trading one warden for another.

"We'll work something out," I promised Kaitlyn.

She nodded sharply, determination tightening her features.

Joss stopped and pointed to a low peak ahead. "There. We need to head past those thinner trees to where the tracker can send out a strong signal."

My chest ached and burned, and Kaitlyn's face was flushed red by the time we reached our pick-up point. Joss sent out the signal and we stood there, waiting, wary at being out in the open. Kaitlyn gave me a helpless look and I smiled at her, hoping to reassure her. But judging from the stiff angle of her shoulders, I didn't think it worked.

It only took moments for the helicopter to arrive. Wind buffeted the dirt, and Ebonguard in full sun-protection rappelled down around us, then scooped us up into the aircraft as swiftly as children scooping up the knucklebones in a game of jacks. We were buckled in and on our way.

I leaned back, watching as the forest dissolved away below us. My heartbeat picked up, a sign of weakness I couldn't fight and hated myself for.

We were being rescued from the wilderness only to be delivered right back into captivity. Back to Umbravallis, a place we'd only just escaped. It was brutally unfair. I had to find a way for us to have a life, a real life, outside all of the darkness and blood and sorrow.

But I might have to become one with the darkness and blood and sorrow to do it.

5

KAITLYN

I had to wonder who was piloting the helicopter, as we flew through the midday sunshine back to the valley of shadows. A human thrall? An Ebonguard flying blind? I wasn't sure which of those ideas I preferred, or if maybe I would rather crash and burn than return to where they were taking us. Maybe they had roped an entirely normal, non-enthralled human pilot into the rescue mission. They'd had some time to arrange things between when the jet apparently made a successful emergency landing back in Umbravallis, and when they picked us up. Maybe it was one of the jet pilots. Could they pilot helicopters too? Would they fly again so soon after all that madness? Maybe the helicopter was autonomous, like the vampires' cars.

The news that the jet had returned safely was all the Ebonguard onboard felt like sharing with us. But it was something. If we were returning to that hellhole, at least I'd have some of my belongings with me, those that hadn't been sucked out of the cabin. I tried to be pragmatic about it all, but we were going to the last place I wanted to be.

The helicopter swooped down low and the sunlight vanished, blocked by the high mountains on either side. Landing at that small airport again, deep in the shadows of Umbravallis, triggered too many memories I'd been ready to leave behind. My lips and nose wrinkled with the effort to fight off nausea, panic, and deep, flaming anger.

The dust settled onto the tarmac, revealing Lance waiting beside a car, looking like he stepped out of an anime. His hair, with its sheer silver sheen that glinted even in the dimmest light, fluttered in the remaining updraft. His chest formed a perfect V-shape, and his legs and arms looked too long for his body. He was powerful despite seeming waiflike, and I knew to think otherwise was stupid and potentially fatal.

He'd been a friend to Owen when they were both vampires, and a friend to us briefly after he'd drunk from me, and my blood had given him a kick of empathy for a short time. But I worried that time was gone. Now, he was the vampire who, under vampire law, owned us. Just what would he do with his belongings when no empathy remained?

I knew that a long time ago, he'd made the choice to be a good man, or a good vampire. He'd even helped Owen make that same choice. But that was before something changed. Owen had told me it was when Lance's choice to spare a human went wrong, and his great-granddaughters were burned at the stake in broad daylight, and all he could do was watch from the shelter of a shadowy corner as they died.

I think, after something like that, his utter lack of give a damn was understandable.

We stepped out of the helicopter, flanked by Ebonguards. Joss remained close to us, and stood out amongst the rest in her makeshift and emergency uniform, rather than the official full sun protection the others wore. Down in the shadows of the vampires' home they'd removed their goggles, but still nothing but their eyes showed.

Lance gave us a cool nod and wry smile. None of us had been expecting to see each other again so soon, and his expression made it clear we'd just dumped unwanted trouble in his lap again.

"Just couldn't keep away, could you?" he asked.

"You know me," I replied. "Walking magnet for misfortune."

He inhaled deeply, and his fangs became visible. "In the brief time you were gone, I'd forgotten how delicious you are. Even knowing the cost to drink, the temptation is almost irresistible." His tone was flirty but his eyes sparkled darkly.

I bristled. My mind screamed that I wasn't food, that he had no right to my body. But my mouth stayed still, fearful.

Joss changed her path from beside me to in front of me, blocking Lance's view of me like a dare. *Just try and get through her.*

Past her shoulder, I could see him taking in her appearance. "Run-in with a Blade? Thought an Ebonguard would have come out of that less scathed than this cat-dragged-in look you have going on right now."

Joss didn't reply, but kept her pace right up until she was nose to nose with Lance. She matched his height and glared silently until Lance cleared his throat and squirmed out of her way.

"Right, then, let's get going." He opened the car door, mumbled something about not being hungry anyway, and let Joss in first. I followed right after, making no effort to hide the smirk on my face.

Owen and Lance got in too, and the driverless car set off down the road.

A sick feeling burbled in my stomach. I didn't know if it was due to pregnancy, terror, the rough night, or some combination of all three. I knew where the car was taking us. There was no other choice I could make with vamps all around us. A *no* could end in our deaths.

The heavy scent of leather filled the car, along with a heavy silence.

Shadows clung thickly to the face of the rocks and the sides of the cliffs that rose up either side of the valley. Little pinpricks of golden light shone from along the smaller side roads, houses and mansions filled with the dead and their slaves.

I closed my eyes to it all. I felt so useless I could barely breathe.

I've survived so much. I'll find a way. I silently chanted the words, but as the car pulled around in front of the palace of the Synedrion, I admitted I was just trying to keep my spirits up.

Wits and sheer luck had gotten me this far, but I couldn't keep relying on them. The only way to be sure to survive was to massively change the balance of power.

I needed to be the powerful one. Somehow.

We were marched without any hesitation or announcement straight into the Synedrion chambers. The leaders of this vampire society waited for us there, up on their thrones of bone-colored limestone. The rest of the assembly hall was empty. No spectators today. Small mercies.

I eyed the seven. Milton, all golden glow and false smile that did nothing to give him the appearance of being friendly or warm. Toren, wrinkled and wizardly.

Bertha, pixie-like and professional in her boyishly slim teenage body. Shirina, clothed in jeweled colors with ebony hair falling and pooling around her ankles. Viatrix, doing her part statue, part ghost impression. Lin, pant-suited, mousy, and practical.

Then the new guy, Dante de Silva. From the moment he threatened us when we first arrived last time, everything about him screamed danger for Owen and me. He was twitchy with barely concealed rage, the kind of rage I'd seen in men who were used to getting their way.

He'd replaced Delphine, who'd died so recently I could still too vividly picture the way her head had parted from her neck. He seemed to me an odd choice for a political ruler, although even in the human world elected leaders frequently confused me. But his installment and position as one of the Synedrion felt like a personal threat directed at Owen and me.

It wasn't just him with the mad face. It was very clear that none of them were happy with us. I was pretty damned unhappy too. I was the one who'd gotten sucked out of a plane, after all. They had lost one of their Ebonguard, but they were there to protect us. Vampires fighting vampire hunters seemed like the natural order that I, a human, had no part in. But here I was, being dragged to the principals' office to take the blame.

Lin spoke first, "Kaitlyn, Owen, I'm afraid we are

going to have to ask you to be our guests for a little while longer."

"Guests my ass," I grunted.

Owen, Lance, and Joss, all by my side, gave me the same look of warning.

"No. You know what? I am sick of you ... you ... people ... vampires. Whatever! Say what you mean. Just say we're your prisoners again."

Dante grinned. "I'll say it. You're our prisoners. You should never have been allowed to leave, not given the new circumstances." He directed the last remark straight at Lin and Shirina. "We should all have been informed of the pregnancy right away."

Oh no.

I'd assumed if Lin and Shirina knew about the pregnancy, then all of the Synedrion did. That we'd been free to go anyway. I should have known better. The respect I found then for Lin and Shirina was overcome by fear of what the others would do with this new knowledge. I dragged in an audible breath, and my hand slid over my stomach reflexively. The way Dante's grin twisted at the sight made me realize it was a mistake to let him know I cared.

Shirina, calm and composed, said, "I'm of the firm opinion that a human woman's body and what happens in it are her own business. I stand by our decision not to share the information."

"Maybe normally, but the prophecy can't be ignored.

This isn't just some human statistic. It could have real, dire implications to our society." Trust Milton to have Dante's back.

Lin took over their defense. "Visions from the chalice are notoriously open to interpretation, and it's clear the pregnancy alone made changes to Kaitlyn's blood that have brought an interpretation of its outcome to pass. It was only after she became pregnant that her blood showed the potential for developing synthetic blood, the solution to our hunger while maintaining our immortality—the promise of the prophecy." She waved a hand. "The offspring itself is unimportant."

Unimportant. The word punched like a bullet into my chest. So much for newfound respect.

"According to you," Dante spat, as elegantly as a child. "But it was not your decision alone to make. I still move that Lin and Shirina be struck from the Synedrion for keeping that information from us."

Bertha's eye-roll was epic. "And nobody has seconded your motion, Dante, so move along yourself and get over it. The pregnancy and prophecy are something we could have monitored from a distance, as I believe Lin and Shirina intended to do anyhow. But the involvement of Alam's Blades has changed things. The implications there are ones we cannot ignore."

Shirina sighed. "Agreed. We can't risk Owen, or especially Kaitlyn, being captured by the Blades. Which is why they are here."

"We could stop their risk of capture by simply terminating them now, if you could all make the right decision," Dante announced.

My muscles went rigid.

"But the prophecy," Bertha mocked in exaggerated worry. "I thought it was important to see that through?"

Dante growled, "More important to see justice."

I watched them arguing for and against us, with little regard for us even being in the room. Even with those arguing for us, it was all semantics over our importance or an understanding of moral guidelines that had no empathy backing it up. All politics and power plays, and no care for our lives.

"I can't." My voice was small but firm. "I can't be prisoner here again. I won't."

"You won't have to," Lance interjected then, stepping forward. "These two are my property. If the Synedrion have decided they must remain in Umbravallis, so be it. But I will keep them, as is my right."

There was silence for a moment, but nods spread across most of the members of the Synedrion—those that moved anyway, Viatrix excluded. Dante and Milton also remained still, but it had clearly been decided.

"You may keep them in your stable," Toren agreed. "Under ongoing Ebonguard watch, of course."

"Stable?" I hissed. "Like animals?"

"He means human stable, with his other thralls and property," Lin clarified, as though that made it better.

I knew, boy did I know, that for most vamps, humans weren't even a step above domesticated livestock.

Dante slunk back in his chair and snarled. "This is ridiculous. Normal rights don't apply here."

Lance's voice was equally cold. "I have claimed them. They're my property now, and I won't take someone trying to steal my property from me with any degree of lightness. Unless you intend to alter claiming rights for all vampirekind, we are done here."

Lance placed one hand on my shoulder and one on Owen's, directing us away. "Let's go."

The council stood, but didn't object. They left their thrones, moving past us, disapproval radiating from each face. As Dante passed, he paused for a moment, smirked at Owen, and said in a voice so soft it was barely audible, "I hope your accommodations are pleasant, and that you will be happy to see some old friends during your stay here."

Owen frowned. I doubted he was in the mood to be catching up with old friends right now, and Dante's pleasant words dripped with malice. The idea of chumming around with vampires made my hairs stand on end. *Owen's not one of you anymore,* I wanted to argue, but Dante's taunt made me question whether maybe Owen wanted to be. Whether he missed his old powers, his old friends, his immortality.

Lance stepped around Dante, ushering us away through a different door. "We really do need to go."

Deathless

We left the palace, and once we were outside again in the crisp and cold air, I grabbed large breaths, trying to cleanse away the anger. I could see blue sky, far above, but no direct sunlight touched anywhere in sight except for the Sun Shrine, a place I didn't want to look. My feet dragged as we followed Lance, and it was only the feel of Owen's hand in mine that kept me steady. I was way past exhausted. I didn't even know if there was a word for how tired I felt. I was so worn out that even my hair hurt.

I'd been sucked out of a plane, had a hard landing, spent the night in a tent, then walked a very long way before being whisked off to this particular corner of hell—and I was starting to feel it. I knew Owen must be too but was scared to mention it because it would just remind him of his mortality.

A slight grin lifted my lips when I recalled the first time he'd caught a cold. He was the worst patient, so dramatic, so pathetic. Like he'd thought he was dying from a rare mutation of the black death every time he'd sneezed. He was wholly offended by the coughing as well, before I assured him it was all normal. Although that memory was cute, the fact that he could be so angry at himself and his body, all the while surrounded by vampires who could give him back his old strength and healing abilities, was not at all cute.

It was flat-out terrifying.

6

KAITLYN

The building Lance lived in would have fit in nicely at the Hamptons. It was a sprawling, three-story mansion, with ornamental gables and large but heavily tinted windows, at least on the first two floors. The third floor appeared to have normal glass, and we were high enough up the slopes of Umbravallis that the mid-afternoon sun just touched those highest windows. The grounds spread out around us, gently rolling hills of lawn which grew patchily from the low light levels and apparent lack of care.

We were met on the wide front porch by the jarring cry of a huge bird, flapping wildly against the insides of its cage.

"Why don't you just let it go?" I said, and for a

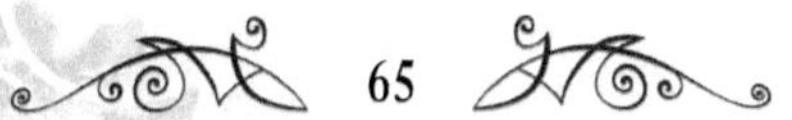

moment I didn't know if I was asking about the bird, or about us.

Lance glanced into the cage, at the fierce predatory eyes glaring back, and the curved beak pulling at the bars. The hawk screamed in frantic protest.

"He was found with a broken wing. It's healed now, but he will never again fly well enough to catch his own food. He knows this, and is aware that if we released him, he would die. But, like all things that could once fly and feed, he misses the feel of wind under his wings and blood in his mouth."

Cold fingers of dread stroked downward into my belly and touched along the base of my spine. My gaze went to Owen. His skin was pale, from exhaustion and stress no doubt, but for a heart-shattering second, he looked so much like the vampire he once was that I couldn't breathe, couldn't think. I grabbed for his hand to feel the warmth of his skin. Only his fingers were chilled from the cold air, and my paranoid dread turned to real fear.

"It just wants to be free," I muttered, as we passed the bird and went inside.

"You know they aren't about to let the two of you go anytime soon. So you might as well settle in." Lance led us through the grand entryway and down a hall, which passed rooms full of books and comfortable spaces, high-tech media and an indulgent indoor pool, and a surprising amount of dust. No kitchens or toilets were to be seen. And I was looking. For both.

Lance seemed to read into my eager peering. "The top floor is set up for humans."

Owen scoffed. "And how many humans do you keep, currently?"

"Just the one, and she's not so much kept, as, well, you'll see."

"Last I knew you had dozens, thralls for every mundane task, and more for food."

Lance's lips grew thin. He turned his back on us and led us toward a tucked away staircase near the corner of the first floor. "I did. After my brush with Kaitlyn's blood, I freed them all. One smack of empathy and now my lawn has gone wild and my house is all dusty."

"You're welcome." I grinned pleasantly.

"Lance? You want me?" a woman called from up ahead.

"I said *dusty*," Lance replied. "But yes. Draw the blinds."

A beep and a swishing sound followed. We rounded the landing on the third floor and stepped straight into an open-plan kitchen and living area, thick curtains blocking out all external light. A woman stood by the counter, remote in one hand, steaming mug in the other, her back to us.

"There you are. It's so late! Thought you'd be hungry."

"I am, but we have guests who must be fed first."

She turned around fast. Her eyes, wide and alert, locked onto us.

Her hair hung long around her, a shade of red so deep it tinted toward purple, neatly brushed, but tattered and uncut at its lengths. Her skin knew sunlight, still pale but not deathly so, with a slim dusting of freckles across her narrow, upturned nose. My eyes went right to her neck. To the hashed mess of scars and fresh bites there. It was the only thing I could see once I looked at them.

She's his strawberry. The words rolled through my head, and sickness quivered up my throat. I wanted to run away from the ravaged skin of her neck. But I also wanted to take her with me. Free her. Save her.

"Oh, hi." She looked caught off guard, and then I saw she was wearing only a T-shirt and panties. My heart galloped. I looked for shackles on her wrists or ankles. *Nothing.* I looked for enthrallment in her eyes. Or fear, desperation. *Nothing.*

"This is Dusky," Lance said. "Dusky, this is Kaitlyn and Owen, they'll be staying here for a while. And Joss, who'll be around as well, keeping an eye on things."

She smiled and waved bashfully while tugging her T-shirt down. "Nice to meet you guys. Uh, if you give me a sec to get dressed, I can cook up something."

"I'd like to cook," Owen said, his expression blank.

"If you don't mind."

"Sure, go ahead. I've already eaten, so just help yourselves. Lance keeps the place stocked with plenty of amazing goodies lately."

Of course he does. He needed Dusky to stay strong, producing fresh blood on demand, so he could feed, and feed, and feed from her. The fanciest of foods for his pet. The sickness came up again, but this time it wasn't in my belly—it was in my heart. But she seemed so … happy? Normal. Not a captive.

"Sort some food out for yourselves then," Lance said. He pointed beyond the simple but comfy lounge area designed to fit a party's worth of people, to a hallway with lots of doorways. "One of the bedrooms is Dusky's, but the rest are empty so take your pick. Bathrooms are at the end. I allow some sunlight in here when it's just humans, but with your Ebonguard on duty, best you keep everything closed up."

"I was getting used to it being just you and me." Dusky seemed put out, pouting and fluttering her eyelashes at Lance.

I eyed the remote in Dusky's hand, wondering if I could grab it, but neither I nor the automated curtains would be faster than an Ebonguard. And I didn't *really* want to do that to Joss.

Maybe Lance though, especially when he said, "Dusky, come with me."

She perked up and trotted after him, a happy

puppy. They went downstairs into Lance's rooms.

When they were gone, I asked through a clenched throat, "He's going to drink from her, isn't he?"

"I imagine so." Owen had begun ransacking the cabinets and the fridge, placing selected ingredients on the counter. "It's hard to see, isn't it?"

"You mean the poor girl being used as a giant slurpee?"

He smiled without a single hint of humor. "It is for me too, all things considered. But he has to feed or die."

My voice held all my bitterness. "Maybe they should all die."

I regretted it immediately, casting a quick "sorry" over to Joss. Despite knowing she was just doing her job, she'd grown on me.

Joss tilted her head. "Would you care if she were a side of beef?"

"She's not a side of beef!"

"No, but cows are living creatures and you eat them. And they aren't even consenting, like Dusky is. Humans eat living creatures, just as much or more than vampires do. And you have other options."

I squirmed, unsure of my own ethical boundaries in the face of monsters. "I keep meaning to go vegan. But bacon."

Joss's eyes squinted slightly. Was there a smile under there? "Some vampires revel in the taking of lives, but many vampires would prefer not to be

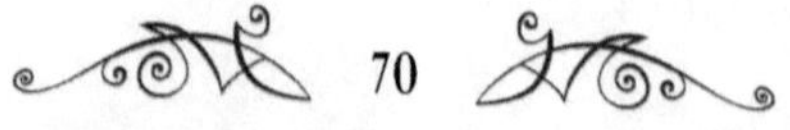

dependent on humans. You and your blood might be the way."

"Does my blood, you know, smell special to you?" I asked. "I mean, are you ever tempted?"

Joss stared me straight in the eye. "Always."

I gulped, and went to the closest window, poking the curtain with just a finger to peek out the gap. Joss stationed herself by the exit doorway, standing as still as a member of the Queen's Guard. I saw her eyes on me, but she didn't react to my curiosity or the tiny beam of sunlight it let in.

We were almost the highest building on the hill, but up a bit higher, along a ceremonial path of shining stone, stood the Sun Shrine. The tortured screams of the Starved that had once echoed from there throughout the valley had stopped, but still echoed in my mind. "Why does he even have so many windows?"

"He doesn't like pasty people," Owen answered.

I blinked a few times. "What?"

He looked up from the pan he was heating on the eight-burner gas range. "He used to say he wanted to give his thralls some quality of life, even as he kept more and more thralls and fewer of his moral guidelines. I'm pretty sure the truth was he just doesn't like pasty-faced servants."

"He should have sent his thralls to get spray tans with Milton, then."

Owen chuckled, tears in his eyes as he chopped onion. "And he thinks people don't know it's fake."

He poured some fragrant olive oil into the pan, then in went the onion with a sizzle, and suddenly, I was starving. I took the first real, deep breath I had for a long time, inhaling the appetizing aroma.

Owen cooked like he was born to do it, and the idea of eating something he made, of sitting down with him to a meal he'd cooked, soothed me.

The kitchen area seemed new and very modern with stainless-steel appliances, dark granite island and countertops, deep farm sinks, and wrought-iron barrel stools pulled up to one bench.

I made my way to his side, where he trimmed bacon and sliced mushrooms. Beside his chopping board was a container of fresh cream, a bottle of white wine, stock, and a brown paper bag rolled down to reveal rustic, handmade pasta. My stomach grumbled in anticipation. "Need some help?"

"Could you find a saucepan and start heating some water?"

I grinned as I searched the cabinets. "You want me to see if there's any tinned tuna?"

His lips peeled off his teeth in an expression of sheer disgust. A flurry of laughter escaped mine, despite everything. That time he'd been sick, I'd tried to make him some comfort food. I'd mixed a tin of tuna into packet mac-n-cheese. It was a go-to back in my poor, struggling actress days. To say he didn't like it was a huge understatement.

"That shall never happen again. I wasn't sure if you were trying to help, or trying to kill me faster. That flu was awful." A vertical slash appeared between his eyebrows, worrying, wondering, then cleared.

"It was barely a sniffle." I elbowed him gently, trying to make light of it, but I worried too. Dante's words floated back to me, seeming like both an offer and a threat.

I found a good-sized saucepan, filled it with hot water, threw in a big pinch of salt, and put it on the stove, then rested my hip against the counter. "Are you looking forward to seeing your old friends? Like Dante said?"

Owen's smoothly stirring hand paused above the frying pan for a moment, then continued. "I'm sure he was just having a go at me. I have no friends here anymore, not since I became human again."

Except maybe Lance. And that Niamh lady who'd met and chaperoned us briefly last time. He could try to deny it but that was at least two friends, or acquaintances.

Maybe I was worried over nothing though. Maybe it was Dante trying to get into our heads.

I tipped the Orecchiette into the boiling water.

"He *did* say it in a creepy voice ... I half expected to hear dramatic organ music playing."

"As he sweeps his cape up over his face, bursts into bats, then flies away over the full moon?" Owen's eyes twinkled.

"You're the one who ran the campy vampire role-playing nights at your club."

He pouted. "I'd thought I was being ironic."

The pasta water overflowed, fizzing on the stovetop. It startled me and I jumped away from it, gasping. Being here, cooking with Owen, felt so normal, so nice, I'd almost forgotten the height of my trauma levels. All it took was a bubbling pot to make me burst into tears.

Owen turned the heat down on both burners and gathered me into his arms. I nestled close and closed my eyes, trying to stop the tears.

"I'm scared," I croaked.

He whispered, "I know. But I'm right here, and no matter what, I'm going to protect you."

What I couldn't say was that I was also scared of the *no matter what*. "No. It's not all on you. I can't let it all be you. It's going to take both of us to save our lives."

I held my breath after I spoke. Owen's pride was as strong as his love for me. I knew how much he wanted—*needed*—to protect me. But he had to know I was right.

He said nothing for a long moment, but the barely perceptible shake of his head was all I needed to see to know he refused to let me share that weight.

Deathless

That he intended to take it all on.

Owen looked deep into my eyes, brushing the hair away from my forehead. "You should go lie down. You're exhausted."

I pulled out of his embrace, frustrated he couldn't agree with me. "The hell if I'm not eating some of this food before I go and sleep."

"Well, I've eaten, so I'm off to bed," Lance announced from the top of the staircase. "Just came back to check everything was sorted before I go."

Eaten. Ugh. A shiver tickled my whole body, and fear for Dusky drove panic into my heart until a moment later, Dusky appeared behind Lance. Her neck was blushed red around fresh puncture marks, and her face wore a dazed, drawn look that I recognized as once being on my own face. It made too many memories hit my brain and heart. I had to distance myself, and fast, from the beginning of my time with Owen. From the time when he wasn't Owen, but Vampire. Out in the human world, I'd learned to set those memories aside, but here, with Dusky's bloody neck in my sight, they pressed in on me, stirring up old pain and resentment. Old trauma that could still break us apart.

"I thought you said you freed all your thralls," I muttered with dripping hatred.

Lance shrugged. "I did free all my thralls, but Dusky ... decided she wanted to hang around."

Dusky smiled in a drunken way at Lance as she slipped by him, her hand circling his waist briefly as she brushed past. He didn't even seem to notice.

Oh ... oh no. My brain finally caught on. Dusky chose to be there. Like I had sought out Owen after he'd freed me. She really was like his Strawberry.

Only Lance didn't love her back. He hadn't become human. He *couldn't* love her back.

"It is super late, guys. See you at nightfall," Dusky mumbled. I didn't know the exact hour—sometime in the mid-afternoon. But she was living on vampire time. She staggered off to what I presumed was her bedroom, with one last puppy-eyed look at Lance before closing the door.

"It is late," Lance agreed. He looked at Joss. "How long have you been on duty without a break?"

"I'm fine." Joss cricked her neck, and stretched one shoulder. The side the branch had gone through.

"Do Ebonguard even take breaks?" I asked, genuinely curious since Joss had become an almost permanent fixture beside me.

"Not usually. But sometimes they do to recover from, say, a dose of Nemexia, branch through the chest, and march through broad daylight," Owen said pointedly while plating up our food.

Lance raised his eyebrows.

"And taking on a vampire hunter with a laser-cannon," I chimed in. "Not to mention that fall

without a parachute. Joss probably saved our lives a half-dozen times. You should have seen how badass she was."

Lance frowned for a moment, taking another look at Joss. "You must need a break. Or some sustenance. I can ask Dusky out again?"

I could have smacked him.

Joss still wore her makeshift mix of daylight coat over the torn-up, skin-tight underlayer of her uniform, and her scarf wrapped around head, but under it all her expression was clear. "I'm perfectly capable of performing my duty. Kaitlyn's safety is my mission. I don't need anything from you."

Lance held his hands up defensively. "Just wanted to be sure you're at your best. You're guarding my property, after all."

"And the get-the-fuck-out award this evening goes to …" I patted the counter in a tiny drumroll while I waited for Lance to take the point.

"All right. I will go then." Lance started leaving but paused to ask again, "You sure? If you want to take an hour or two rest downstairs, I can stay with them."

Joss ignored him, still and at attention. Lance left.

I took the plate Owen handed me and started shoveling food into my mouth. I was sure it was delicious, but I couldn't taste a single thing except for the salt that lay in the back of my throat.

Another Ebonguard came to relieve Joss. He didn't bother introducing himself, but I heard Joss call him Heim. He was brusque, even compared to her. He seemed to speak down to her. I already didn't like him. Apparently, he was now in charge of our safety—mine, particularly. He brought with him thralled servants who delivered our remaining luggage from the plane. Joss left.

Owen's fingers brushed mine, and I looked up from a plate I didn't remember emptying. His face wore lines of fatigue and his hair was rumpled. "Bed?"

I slumped onto the counter, staring blankly at the litter of our dinner. I didn't want to sleep. I wanted to fight and prepare and plan.

But everything hurt, and I couldn't stop yawning. "Bed."

We picked a room at random. They were all equally bland, clean, and sparse, like budget hotel rooms. But the bed was an actual bed, rather than a foil-thin sleeping bag on the ground. Curling up together in any bed would have felt wonderful, and my whole body sighed.

Owen snuggled up against me. "You okay?"

I wanted to be strong and profess my okay-ness but for real, I was not okay. Really not okay. "Nope. You?"

"No."

I closed my eyes, my head swimming with sleep. "What are we going to do?"

"Try to escape."

"Of course," I replied. "Because it will be so easy."

Even if we lost our bodyguards and got clear of Umbravallis somehow, we would be hunted, and no place was safe or far enough away from these vampires. "We could use a backup plan."

Owen hummed, a thinking sound, and it tickled against my ear. "Try to cooperate, gain some leverage, and see if we can somehow lessen their influence on our lives?"

"Totally doable."

7

KAITLYN

I snapped from the blank nothingness of total exhaustion to alert panic some hours later. My body needed more rest, but my brain was in overdrive. Owen lay beside me, deep in sleep, and I envied how peaceful he looked. After futilely lying still for twenty minutes, I got up and peered out a curtain. Nighttime. The moon was sliced down the middle, half light, half dark, and insects chirped away in the long grass. I peeked out our bedroom door. The lights were all on, there were voices in the living area, and Heim stood on guard right beside my snooping face.

He followed me and my bundle of clothes and toiletries down the hall to the bathroom, but thankfully stayed outside. A shower, fresh clothes, and toothpaste returned some of my humanity. In my

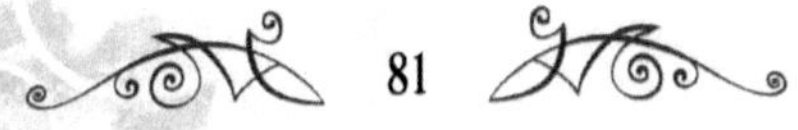

luggage, I also found the small history book Lance had given me before we left. Maybe I could learn some more about vampires from it. *Leverage.* That was what I needed in this world of power plays. And that started with knowledge. I pocketed it and went out to the stable's common area, Heim remaining a few paces behind all the way.

I heard the clash of steel on steel, and my heart skipped a few beats. My first thought was that we were under attack again, like the night with the Starved. Maybe it would be the Overfed this time. I saw Lance circling an Ebonguard on the largest rug of the room, sword drawn. It was Joss. I knew her by her eyes now. She'd returned, uniform clean and intact.

"What'd you do to piss her off this time?" I asked Lance.

Lance gave me a swash-bucklingly handsome smile. "I wanted to see just how good an Ebonguard was, up close. Joss agreed to show me some of her tricks."

I took a seat on the gray modular lounge next to Dusky to watch. The curtains were all drawn open, showing the starry night through the large windows, the perfect backdrop for the show.

Joss's movements were formal and lightning-fast. She struck at Lance, lethal blows she pulled back on at the very last moment. He tried to dodge or block her with an antique sword he'd probably pulled from a wall downstairs. He only saved his own life one in every four strikes with the sound of ringing metal. He seemed more thrilled than frustrated at his defeats. His silver hair swished around his growing smile.

Dusky sighed deeply. "I swear he's so hot I just want to die. Don't you think so?"

"Yeah, I s'pose." She'd been fed from, and recently. I looked away, trying not to see the raw and red wounds on her flesh. I did think she wanted to die. The evidence to back up that belief was carved into her flesh.

"It must be so amazing to be one of them."

"A vampire?"

"You never wanted Owen to make you into one? Before you changed him?" There was a level of distaste to those last words.

Shudders ran all along my skin. Of course, immortality was alluring, but the price, in my mind, was always too high. Sure, some vampires could pass as human casually, and maybe calling them all evil was taking it too far. But I'd seen evil right up close. I'd heard it speak through lips stitched shut and looked into its dried and dead eyes.

"No. I never wanted that."

Dusky gushed, "I want to be one *so bad*, but Lance won't make me into one no matter how much I beg, and neither will any of the others, because they don't want to piss him off."

"I wonder if they have some kind of quota. Like they are only allowed to turn a certain number of humans to vampires each. Like a single-child policy. Otherwise, you'd think they'd quickly turn the whole world to vamps and end up with nothing left to eat." It wasn't necessarily comforting to Dusky, but I couldn't help thinking out loud.

Dusky shook her head. Her tone broke my heart. "He just doesn't like me. I know it. But it's because I'm human. If he'd just turn me, if I could just be like him, I could be his equal, and then maybe he could look at me the right way."

I wanted to reassure her, but I didn't know what I could say and sound sincere. I watched Lance and Joss go at it, and uneasiness sparked into my being. There was tension between the two of them, and it wasn't homicidal—it was all sexual. I looked over at Dusky. Her lips were pursed and her eyes narrowed. Her voice was high and thin. "I don't know why he wants to spend so much time with her. I swear she's just like … I mean, she's just …"

Joss was strong, confident, loyal, and smart. All of that added up to her being sexy as hell, even when you could only see her eyes. Eyes Lance couldn't look away from.

They were locked in a tense embrace. Despite holding weapons, it looked more like foreplay than warfare. I bet it looked the very same way to Dusky, and I bet it hurt.

I sympathized. I fell in love with Owen, even though he fed from me. I told myself I grew to love the human who slowly emerged, all the while hating the vampire who fed from me and kept me prisoner, but could I truly completely separate those two entities?

Even when I loved him, I still wanted to flee, because I knew I wasn't safe. Dusky had to know that at some point Lance could drink too much and kill her. Whether by accident or design, it wouldn't matter. The result would be the same.

"If you're free to leave, you should go. This isn't the place for humans," I said.

"I kno-ow," she sang. "That's why I've got to become a vampire to be with him."

If you become a vampire, he won't need you anymore. I wanted to say it, make her realize the truth, and run far away. But it felt too cruel.

She seemed to read my silence and expression as equally cruel. "I'll find a way." Her eyes narrowed, and she huffed off.

Lance paused, watching Dusky go. He said something to Joss, and they broke apart. He came over to me, skin matte and fresh, not a broken sweat or labored breath to indicate he'd just been fighting.

"I need to do something with her." He grimaced, like Dusky was an unwanted pet he'd dumped out in the woods that kept bringing itself home.

"You could try not drinking her blood," I snapped.

He shrugged. "She offers."

"Of course she does! She's a vampire groupie in general, and a Lance groupie in particular. You must know she's in love with you, and she thinks you care for her because you keep feeding from her." There it was again, a truth uncomfortably close to my past slapping me in the face at every turn. "She's going to keep sticking around because you keep feeding from her and giving her the hope that one day, you're going to turn her and declare your undead undying love."

"I have to feed from someone. Why shouldn't it be someone free and willing?"

"Because infatuation can be just as much of a prison as enthrallment. It'd be hard to re-integrate into society after what you've put her through. If you cared at all about her, you would stop taking her blood and give her some walking papers. Maybe a nice memory wipe while you're at it. Set her up in some sweet little apartment and give her compensation income until she gets it together."

Lance stared at me blankly for a long moment. "I've forgotten how to care. Centuries of letting myself make no effort in moral regards have made it hard to make correct decisions anymore. Maybe you're right. But maybe you aren't. Humans have so many feelings about everything, and you could just be projecting your own feelings onto her. Dusky seems happy enough."

"For now," I muttered. I didn't even know why I cared. If Dusky wanted to fangirl the vamps, maybe that was her business. But it hurt to watch her give her blood so willingly. It made me sick, because it brought home what I might have become had my blood not changed Owen.

I walked away from Lance and the lounge and went over to Joss. She had continued to run through a series of martial arts stances on her own.

She paused when I stood in front of her.

"Can you train me to fight?"

A single strand of pink hair edged into the open eye area of Joss's head covering, shaken loose. She squinted at me. "You're pregnant."

"So you expect me to spend the next nine months lying in bed?"

Joss shrugged. "It's been a long time since I was around a pregnant human.

"Well, it's not like that these days. I still have a fully functioning body right now."

That squint again.

Lance announced from across the room, "I have to head down to the Synedrion estate. Been summoned for an update on the humans, no doubt. I'll be back shortly."

Joss and I both replied with a grunt.

I waited for Lance to walk out, leaving Joss and I alone, except for Heim stationed like a robot by the exit door.

"Come on," I pleaded. "I did some stunt training for my acting—fight choreography—so I already know the basics."

Joss laughed. She actually laughed out loud, in my face.

I was caught so off guard I asked, "Are you okay?" Between the laughter and her moving freely around the room, sparring with Lance and generally showing freewill, I'd become concerned.

"I'm off-duty. This is my recuperation break, not my train-the-civvies time."

"If you're off-duty, why are you here?"

Joss glanced across at Heim, then back to me. She shrugged. "I was returning to duty here in the morning anyway—"

"As second," Heim felt the need to interject.

Joss didn't continue her thought, just stared at Heim.

He stared back. "I am in charge of the female human's protection now. And there are plenty of Ebonguard stationed around the property. You aren't required here."

"But you are appreciated," I said. I liked Joss, as much as I could like a vampire. I would have much preferred she remain my bodyguard than the new guy.

With a sniff, Joss turned back to me. "You want to train to fight?"

"Sure do." I lifted my fists, ready to go.

Joss still wasn't sold. "Why?"

Why? I had so many reasons they rushed my mouth like a crowd stampeding a doorway, all getting stuck in there, none getting free. My hands patted my belly, trying to soothe the quivering. Just nerves, but part of my brain felt like the anxious flutter and lift in my gut was my child reacting to danger, asking for protection from it.

Joss answered for me. "You're afraid you'll be killed."

"Wouldn't you be if you were me?"

"No. I … *we* are here to guard you."

"And what happens when your orders change? If you are the one ordered to kill me?"

Her eyes held no expression. "Then you will die."

There it was. I couldn't expect Joss's loyalty to be given to me. She was loyal to her kind, her cause. She was here doing her duty, even off the clock, because she was proving herself to her superiors. I knew she'd already failed in the past, already hit two strikes on the Ebonguards' three-strike system. And I knew she'd follow any order to not be struck out.

But for now, she was ordered to protect me, and

I could use that. "Then while we're on the same side, I want you to train me, so I have some chance on my own."

"You know there's no way you could ever win against me in a real fight."

"You know if we ever got into a real fight, I'd do everything, anything, to survive."

"I do." Her head bowed in the slightest nod. "And I respect that. But you could change everything. Our entire world. For better or for worse. I don't intend to let you go. I'll help train you, but don't mistake that as my being weak."

"I'd never think you were weak. Not after what we've been through together." It felt like we were exchanging some strange wedding vows. "But I still want to be able to protect myself, and this baby. I have to. I can't let it grow up in a prison, captive, like this. We have to have our freedom."

Joss paused, sniffed, then tucked her errant strand of hair out of sight. "I can understand that." She moved back into one of her stances. "Okay. We'll start simple."

I copied her pose and managed a smile. "Simple's good."

But would it be good enough?

8

OWEN

I was a prisoner to my dream. Too tired to wake, too aware to ignore the horror. Fangs and blood, screams and pain. Suffering dealt out by my hands, my teeth, bloody gifts given to a woman by me. Not just any woman either.

Kaitlyn.

I sat up. My hands wiped my sweaty face as I tried to get my breathing under control. The very need to breathe, and how panic could overtake control of that and other functions, was so new to me.

Panic again set in when it hit me that she wasn't there. My eyes still blurred with sleep, and I patted at the sheets and mussed covers like I was going to find her huddled down within them, but all I felt was the cool mattress.

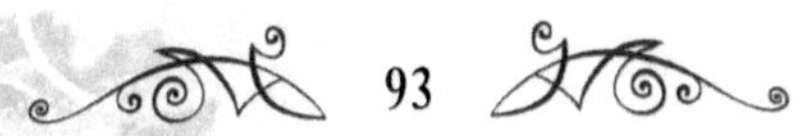

"Kaitlyn?"

No answer. The sheets tangled around my body as I swung my feet free of the bed and grabbed at the pants I'd left on the floor. Where was she? All I knew was she wasn't in here with me—she was out there. With Lance?

Jealousy zoomed into my being, and I couldn't shatter it any more than I could shake off the last terrible vestiges of that dream. Whatever Lance might feel for Kaitlyn, she didn't reciprocate that feeling. She loved me. Wanted nobody but me.

I still reeled with jealousy.

I pulled my pants up and buttoned them, then stopped to take a breath. Why? Why was I so upset when I knew how she felt about me?

Because he could protect her.

My heart raced, and my hands shook as I tried to work past the nightmare, to get it to loosen its hold, to let me think clearly.

I'd had that dream more than I'd like to admit— but it wasn't all dream. It was part memory. Part fear of *what if?* What if I had killed Kaitlyn when I held her captive, when I drank so greedily from her?

What if her blood had not turned me human and she still suffered?

What if I was no better as a human than I was as a vampire?

What if I became a vampire again?

A sour taste grew in my mouth. I flung open the curtains. Still nighttime, but the barest hints of dawn had chased the stars away. I stepped out of our room and down the hallway.

The loungeroom was lit up, and Kaitlyn was there. Safe. Wearing pajamas and mirroring Joss's movements as they kickboxed their way across the rug. The sight of her calmed me, and I leaned on the wall, watching.

"You look like hell." Lance's voice turned me to him. He had just walked in, dressed in a full suit, making me feel awkward in my disheveled pants-only look.

"This place is hell, so I'm fitting in." I knew my words were rude. I couldn't bring myself to hold back.

"Hardly," Lance replied, whether to this place being hell or to me fitting in, I didn't know.

I regarded him carefully. We could use an ally, I just wasn't sold on the idea that our ally would be Lance. He'd told me Kaitlyn's blood had changed him, reminded him what it was to choose a moral path again. Him claiming us as his humans had saved us from being claimed by some other—probably worse—vampire. But any change from her blood was now gone. No true empathy remained. He was just as mired in the politics of this world as the rest of them, and if something didn't serve his agenda, it didn't matter. The real question was, what did he want from me? Or, really, what did he want from Kaitlyn? Drinking from her could turn him human. He didn't want that, but that didn't mean he didn't crave her blood. It was like a siren's call. I knew how hard it was to resist.

Kaitlyn glanced over then, noticing me. I saw her eyes look over my shirtless chest, and the small smile it brought her.

Lance elbowed me. "No need to worry about your style, we'll have you fitting in again soon. There's a masquerade ball next-night."

Kaitlyn joined us, patting at her sweaty forehead with the back of her hand. "A masquerade?"

I managed a taut smile. "Vampires do love their masquerades."

"You're to go, both of you." Lance drew two cards from his suit pocket. "Invitations direct from Dante de Silva."

"Gross," Kaitlyn said. "Another mandatory invitation, right?"

"Of course." Lance grinned.

"Of course," Kaitlyn echoed, deadpan.

"Kaitlyn has also been requested to see Lin and Shirina in the lab the morning after. So we will have an excuse to leave before the party gets too wild."

I took the invitations off Lance, frowning. I was more worried about our safety with Dante and his grudge against me than the threat of Alam's Blades.

Deathless

The careful calligraphy told me the party started tomorrow evening, and would no doubt go until the early hours. Getting used to vampire time was a pain, but even having just woken up, I was sure Kaitlyn and I could easily sleep through another day. I longed to be curled around her again. It was the only time I could pretend we were both safe, in a bubble together that nothing could burst.

I moved toward her and slid an arm around her waist. Her body was hot to touch, and her face flushed with a sheen of sweat. Concern swamped me. "Are you all right?"

"Might need another shower."

"I mean, is the exertion good for the baby?" I genuinely had no idea. I was sure the treatment of pregnancy had changed greatly since the last I'd cared to know anything about it. I was sure I remembered something about women needing to stay still so the baby wasn't shaken free of their bodies. I really needed to read some modern books.

She gave me a look. "I was being careful."

Of course she was. "I know. I just worry."

"I know." She popped up on her tiptoes and kissed me on the cheek.

Lance cleared his throat. "I'll have some outfits sent for you both. See you at nightfall."

"Good night," Kaitlyn said, not looking away from me. "Or good morning, whatever it is."

My eyes didn't leave hers either as we made our way back to the room we'd claimed.

I knew she was out there training with Joss because she wanted to protect us, all of us. But no training in the world would save a human from a pack of pissed off vampires.

Alam's Blades were human. At least, most of them. But they had weapons like I'd never seen, and they knew what to do with them. Maybe I could align us with the hunters, but doing that would set us at serious odds with the vampires and might be the thing that got Kaitlyn and our child killed.

When we reached our room, a comfortable silence crept in. I pulled Kaitlyn tight to me, and the touch of her skin stirred up desire. I would always want her. Always. Her body was real and solid against mine. Warm and alive. Our lips met, and hers tasted like salt. Birds sung their morning chorus out on the windy hills around us. Through the open curtains, the sun hung cradled in the high mountains, gifting us with a single thin beam of light.

I didn't want to give this up. I didn't want to stand away from the sunlight, hidden in the shadows. I didn't want to reverse my life yet again and become a creature of darkness.

But this wasn't about what I wanted. It was about her. Everything was for her, and our baby.

9

KAITLYN

The masquerade was in full swing when we arrived at the Synedrion palace. Lance had ensured we arrived late—fashionably, but not enough to annoy our hosts.

The cave that housed the estate was lit up bright, floodlights making the stalactites translucent and milky, hanging above us like giant teeth. Revelers swarmed the grounds and palace entrance, and all eyes turned to us as we stepped out of our ride. More teeth were showing.

"A little help?" I said, halfway out the car door. I was stuck, my gown far too impractical for a car. I felt like I required an open-top horse-drawn carriage to float elegantly down from upon arrival. But horses shied away from vampires, so there was no carriage to be had.

Owen took my hand, trying to help me wiggle free without tearing the dress. The gown was impossibly pretty but built like a torture device. The corset was so tight I was going to spend the entire night hoping I didn't breathe so deeply my breasts popped out. The skirt was made from yards upon yards of rich red satin, twisted into rose shapes, and it was so heavy it had to be held out by a crinoline cage.

I could almost imagine the champagne cork sound effect as I popped free from the car. Owen caught me in his arms as the momentum toppled me forward.

"At least I can save you from costume malfunctions," Owen said wryly.

"You legit jumped out of a plane for me, so you're good in the hero books. But I wouldn't turn down trading outfits if you wanted to save me again." I eyed his puffy white shirt, brocade jacket, and skintight gray breeches. *Yeah, I could pull that off.*

"Red *is* my color," Owen mused. The smile reached his eyes, even behind his barn owl-themed mask.

"No outfit trading," Lance called from a few paces ahead. "We're already late." He could talk, in his far more modern suit in a subtle metallic silver. Dusky, standing a step behind his shoulder, also got away with a simple slimline evening gown in muted purple.

Joss and Heim, at our backs, still wore their usual black uniforms, but most of the other party-goers were wearing what seemed to be period costumes, ranging from Renaissance, to French Revolution, to Victorian. Like they were reliving their heydays.

I grumbled a sigh.

Owen shrugged and hooked my arm in his, leading us inside. "I never enjoyed wearing this stuff, even when it was modern and fashionable."

That thought made me cold. He *had been* alive when these clothes were in fashion. It was overwhelming, that he actually had memories of a time that seemed like fiction me. "At least your clothes are practical."

My heart hurt. I hated this. I hated being forced to go to a party with our captors. I hated being forced to relive a history I never knew and didn't really want to know either.

I hated that this all brought home just how wide the gulf between Owen and I really was.

We stepped into the main building, then through to the grand ballroom where the party was underway. Dancers were all over the floor, a confection of swirling fabric and glitter and masks. A chamber orchestra played something classical yet upbeat, but the musicians all wore blank, fixed expressions. Tables laden with the most decadent-looking cakes and tiered treat towers lined the edges of the space, untouched, while vampires fed on enthralled humans instead.

I wanted out, even though we'd just got there.

I reached a hand to my face, feeling the mask

of red feathers, velvet, and white pearls. Only my lips and chin were visible underneath it, and my eyes shadowed through small holes. The feathers splayed out wide and high over my hair piled on top of my head. That I was almost unrecognizable didn't matter. Every vampire there would be able to smell my blood.

And from the looks on their faces, they did.

I turned my back on the room and beelined for a food table. I wasn't hungry since we ate before we left, but the food table was always my go-to sanctuary at awkward social gatherings.

Owen crushed my hopes. "I wouldn't eat any of that. It's all decorative."

"No cake?" I poked a towering gateau and found under the heavy layer of gummy fondant it was nothing but polyfoam. "Kill me now."

"I could probably rustle you up a glass of water?" he offered.

"We should have BYOed. I could badly use a glass of wine. Just one. I'm sure it would be fine." Inner guilt shook its head at me. "Maybe half a glass. *Fine.* Water."

Owen began unlooping his arm from mine, and I clung onto him. "On second thought, just stay with me?"

He squeezed my hand, then let go. "You'll be fine. I'll be fine. I'll get you some water."

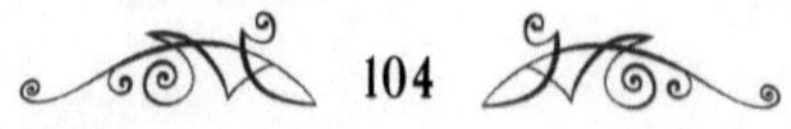

Deathless

As he stepped away, Joss split off and followed him too. Heim remained near me, always nearby. Even here I had to be protected. Maybe especially here.

The vampires knew I was out of bounds, but they watched me regardless, avidly. Given the chance, I was sure they'd take a bite of the forbidden fruit.

"Night's greetings to you all." Niamh swanned up to us, arms wide in a non-embrace as she leaned in to peck Lance on each cheek. She seemed ready to do the same to me, but thought better of it. "I heard you were back with us again, Miss French. Owen too?"

"Yeah. He's around." I looked up and down the great height of the blond beauty. One of Owen's *old friends*. I glanced around behind her, and also spotted Milton and Bertha, enjoying themselves among the dancers. Dante watched from the nearby corner. *No welcome from our inviter? What a shame.*

Lance and Niamh continued their small talk, and I turned away to find myself face to face with Dusky. Her eyes glittered through the holes carved into her satin mask. "Isn't this amazing?"

"The best." I admired her enthusiasm but couldn't control my sarcasm.

She missed my tone, apparently, because she beamed. "It's so magical! I've been to some masquerades before. I think. But not like this." Her gaze flicked over to a vampire feeding on a human nearby. "I don't

really remember. It's hard to remember everything from when I was enthralled. Either way, I couldn't really enjoy it like I can now. Thank you."

"Thank me?"

"Didn't you talk Lance into letting me come?"

Had I? If I had, he really didn't get the right message. Maybe he just invited her because he knew she'd be pissed if he took his new humans to the ball without her.

I shrugged, passing off my confusion as modesty. She bumped her shoulder against mine like a silent thank you, and my heart ached for her.

The music changed and a cheer rang out. The orchestra played like they were possessed, because they were. Sweat and exhaustion dripped from them, but they couldn't slow, couldn't stop. Resentment sizzled along my nervous system.

Dusky grabbed my arm and dragged me forward. "Let's dance. It will be fun!"

I wanted to say no, but in a way, this was Dusky's Cinderella night. Her time to be included. Her time to be seen and feel special after so much hardship. As the only other free-willed human woman there, I couldn't say no to her.

I managed a smile as Dusky hauled me out into the crowd of predators. Waves of perfume, cologne, and that ever-present coppery scent assaulted me. I checked back to see if my Ebonguard still had eyes on me, comforted that he did. But the crowd swirled. Glittering jewels and sparkling fabrics spun and created a haze between us.

Dusky glowed with joy as she squeezed into her position in the women's row, and I giggled as I took a spot opposite her in the men's row. I laughed even harder when I realized I had no idea of any of the dance moves all the vampires followed, but it became clear that neither did Dusky, so we just did our best to copy along and ad lib when needed.

I was almost having fun, caught up in the rhythm of movement, until everybody shifted along, swirled about, and partners were swapped. The female vampire I came face to face with was caught as much by surprise as I was. I tried to step away and twirl myself back to Dusky, or off the dancefloor entirely.

I pinballed from one place to another. Laughter rose, and passing me from vampire to vampire seemed to become a game. Everywhere I looked there were diamonds and lace, pearls and taffeta. No escape. My heart pounded furiously as I swiveled right with the other dancers to face my next partner.

She wore a stunning gown of ice blue, cinched in tightly at the waist, her skin as pale as the gown. She seemed amused, probably because I was delivered to her instead of a male dancer.

"I was in the wrong line, sorry," I gasped, trying to back away.

Black eyes peered out from behind a mask covered in so many brilliant diamonds it was hard to look at. "I'm happy to lead, if you prefer."

Her smile was pleasant, and I sighed with relief as she switched places with me. One small humiliation dealt with. But as all the other men bowed to their partners, she caught me up in her hands, ignoring the choreography.

Her fingers, strong and so very cold, gripped mine, and she swept me deeper into the sea of dancers. My feet stumbled, and she caught me expertly. A bad feeling settled in. I felt like a mouse that almost got away. But *almost* never really counts.

I tried to keep pace, keep a smile on my face, and wait for the next partner change.

The music swelled, and we were moved by the bodies surrounding ours. The dance had become too fast, beyond human speed, and I couldn't keep up. I couldn't catch my breath. The gown, so heavy, and billowing out all around me, kept sending me off balance. The vampires all moved freely in their tight and heavy gowns. Weight and breath meant nothing to them. Their feet were fleeting, and their bodies moved in sharp and precise motions. Partners changed, but the icy woman didn't let me go.

I gave up the effort to smile, to be polite. I yanked hard, trying to get my hand out of her frozen grip. She pulled me close, chest to chest like we were lovers dancing. Her breath, smelling of tangy blood, washed over my face. She spoke, seductive and poisonous in my ear. "He lied to you."

"What? Who?"

Her smile was all fangs and blood-red lips. "Our precious Owen. He's lied to everyone about how I died."

I was lost. "How you became a vampire?"

She peered at me with fevered eyes. "He thought me gone forever. Destroyed. He was wrong. Now I can tell everyone how he killed me. With Tiamat's ring."

I shook my head, tried to shake my body free. "The cursed ring? It chooses its victims." And killed them. It killed Harvey. It killed …

"No!" I gasped.

"Oh, you do know me." Her laughter was a whisper of sheer malice. She ran her nose along my neck, inhaling my fear. "You do smell so delicious. It will be a delight to remove something so special from Owen's life. You tell him. Tell him I'm returned, and that I will destroy him, you, and all he holds dear."

Horror coiled inside me, and I unleashed a scream that shook the chandeliers above us. "JOSSSSS!"

It didn't matter that Heim was my protector now. Or that my heart was screaming for Owen. It was Joss my mouth cried out for. My hands clawed and punched at the woman but in the next moment I was freed, and she was swirling away in Dante's arms.

My scream had stopped the music, and the entire

crowd stared at me for the fraction of a second it took for half a dozen Ebonguard to circle around me.

I was scooped off my feet, taken off the dancefloor. The one carrying me asked, "What happened?" *Joss.*

My insides churned. My heart slammed into overdrive and my mouth went dry. "Something bad. Where's Owen?"

"I'll take you."

I had to talk to Owen before I talked to anyone else.

Because Owen's ex-girlfriend was back from the dead and out for revenge.

10

OWEN

I made my way back, a champagne flute of water in each hand, to find Lance chatting with Niamh, and Kaitlyn and Dusky gone. It had taken me some time to find the glasses, and I'd had to go all the way into the thralls' kitchens for drinking water. I'd hated leaving Kaitlyn for those long minutes, but I wanted to make a show that things were somehow *okay*. They really weren't, but the act of going to get my partner a drink at a party should have been okay. It was a small freedom I wanted for us.

I put the flutes down on a table and looked around for Kaitlyn. Heim remained at attention, watching the dancers, and Joss had my back, so I tried to calm the nerves that rose at finding Kaitlyn absent. If anything was wrong, they would be on it. Kaitlyn

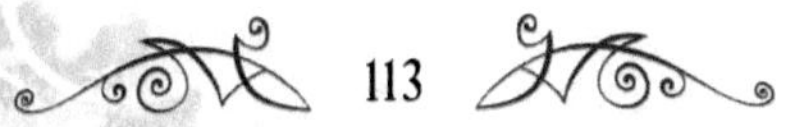

was probably just—

Joss sprang into action, speeding off so fast she left only a black blur. Heim followed. My heart went with them because their action could only mean something was wrong with Kaitlyn.

I hadn't realized I was trying to run after the Ebonguard until the force of Lance's hands on my shoulders started to ache. He forced me into a corner of the room.

Then Ebonguard appeared all around us, a small army of black. One of them carried Kaitlyn in their arms, a mountain of rose-red fabric piled all around. She was placed back on her feet and stumbled straight into my arms. I felt her whole chest lift and sigh in relief.

Then she separated herself from me and shoved me with both hands. Her expression was wary, her skin as pale as death.

"What is happening?" I asked.

She glanced at the wall of Ebonguard surrounding us, Lance and Niamh and half the ballroom listening in. "Nothing. I'm fine. I just ... I was dancing and I panicked and can-we-go-some-where-private-like-right-now-okay?"

The words spilled from her shaking lips in a rapid tumble. I nodded, then led her through the nearest exit door. I knew the Ebonguard would be right behind us, but at least we'd be away from the gawking crowd.

The doors opened out into a small side chamber sitting room of dark wood, ancient books, and velvet lounges. A vampire was feeding on a human in the corner, but one look at us and our entourage had the two of them clearing out.

We went to the opposite corner, as far from the Ebonguard as they'd allow. Kaitlyn moved a tasseled floor lamp out of our way and placed it in front of us, as though we could have hidden behind it.

She yanked her mask off, and her eyes were wide and frightened. Her voice was a low hiss. "Adelle is alive. She's here. She danced with me, and she threatened to destroy you and everything you care about."

"Adelle? Adelle St Delaurents? That's who she said she was?"

"No, she didn't exactly introduce herself formally, but I know it was her." Kaitlyn's fingers grabbed at my sleeve, tearing away a slim strip of lace.

I took her hands, trying to calm her. "Adelle is dust. It must have been someone else. Someone trying to scare us."

"Oh." It was a long, drawn-out syllable of under-standing. "She was with Dante, left with Dante. Is that what he meant? Is this all him? No, this was definitely personal to her too. I could see it in her eyes."

I had no idea what she was talking about but could clearly see she was shaken. "Slow down. Tell me what happened."

Kaitlyn took a long breath. "I ended up dancing with this vampire. All icy blond bombshell. She seemed nice at first, but it got bad real fast."

"That certainly sounds like Adelle." But Adelle was undeniably dead. Her earlier words sank in. "Wait. What did you mean when you asked if this was what Dante meant?"

"Remember him being all ominous about meeting an old friend? Could this be him playing with us?"

"Maybe. That's why she went for you. If it was an imposter, I would have picked her straight away, but dropping a few clues with you would be enough to rattle us. What exactly did she say?"

Kaitlyn lowered her voice, so low I could barely hear her. "She said you killed her. With Tiamat's ring."

Tiamat's ring. I was punch-drunk, swaying on my feet as though those words had knocked me cold. This wasn't a trick or a set-up. This wasn't a mistake. Kaitlyn was right. It had to be Adelle. Only Adelle and I knew what had happened that night. Dante claimed to have seen, hiding in the room like the jealous lover he was, but even he didn't know what I'd retrieved from Adelle's ashes. Or did he? I'd thought only Adelle knew I gifted her the ring, only she had seen it right before it took its effect and had been able to identify it for what it was. The ring I was not supposed to have, and yet did and still do.

"Owen?"

"Huh?"

"What does that mean? Did you—?"

I halted her words with a kiss. There was a chance she'd be overheard, if she hadn't been already. Vampires didn't have better hearing than normal humans, but these days, for all I knew, Kaitlyn and I were bugged. Dread rolled through me like a snowstorm. If it really was Adelle, and it seemed to be, I was as good as dead. Whether she claimed her revenge on me herself, or revealed the truth of my crime, it didn't matter. Adelle loved to destroy things, and loved to destroy me most of all.

Kaitlyn watched my face with growing horror. "It's true, isn't it? It is *her*. And you did—"

"I want to tell you everything, but I can't. Not here."

I had to tell Kaitlyn what really happened to Adelle. It was a secret I'd intended to take beyond the grave, but if Adelle was back, that changed everything. All my lies and stories, the fiction I'd created, was going to fall apart, and Kaitlyn deserved to hear the truth from me.

"Tell me now." She crossed her arms and her eyes flashed dangerously.

I scanned our surroundings, checking the Ebonguard still across the room. They looked put out at the big fuss Kaitlyn had made, and that we now appeared to be either canoodling in a corner or having a spat, or both. If they'd been listening in, I'd be done already.

I pressed my cheek to hers and whispered in her ear, "Don't let the Ebonguard know anything is wrong. I'll tell you everything."

I leaned into Kaitlyn and gathered her close. Her body was rigid and didn't fit against mine. "The ring, the cursed ring of silver with the tear-drop ruby—I lied about it. It doesn't choose its victims like I said, it must be gifted to the victim. It is an artifact with the power to cause untraceable death. The perfect murder weapon." Unless it turned out there was a hidden witness, like Dante. But even then, he could prove nothing. Until now.

"So you killed Adelle with it on purpose?" Her whisper was shaky.

I nodded. She already knew I had sought Adelle's death, but after that she believed a cursed ring chose Adelle to die. Now Kaitlyn knew how direct my part was in her death, she looked at me differently.

"Do you still have the ring?"

I nodded again.

She pouted. "You have a magic ring and you didn't tell me?"

"I didn't tell you because I didn't tell *anyone*. I can be killed just for having it. It's *Tiamat's* ring, a sacred object that belonged to one of the original seven. To possess it and not turn it over to the

Deathless

Synedrion—that alone is a crime punishable by death, no matter if you are a vampire or a human."

She sniffed a harsh breath. "And it's against the law for a vamp to kill another vamp. A crime you get bound to the sun for. And she knows you killed her. When you were both vampires. With that ring. That you shouldn't have."

I didn't even nod, just looked her in the eyes as it all settled on her.

"Oh man, we're screwed."

A wry smile quirked my lips. "I know. For now, the ring is hidden, but if I could get it back, if I could use it on her again before she told anyone—"

Kaitlyn's head shook as she laughed dryly. "I can't believe we're actually at the point of planning murder by magical ring. Is this really where our lives are right now?"

"What else can we do? She's a vampire. A dangerous one. And we're humans."

"I know. I just hate that this is what we've come to: forced into kill-or-be-killed situations. You're not a vampire anymore, Owen. Killing shouldn't be your go-to solution."

I wanted to say it wasn't, but every nerve inside me cried out for bloody carnage. Death had been part of my world for so long, it had become so normalized. But that didn't make it right.

Kaitlyn huffed. "I get the need for self-defense.

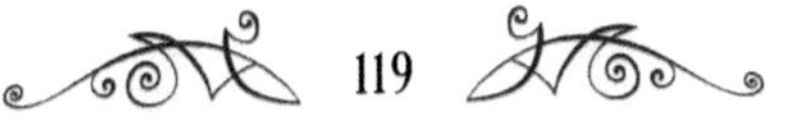

I get needing to do whatever we have to do to stay alive, but if only we could do that some other way. A deterrent, like the Nemexia."

"If we could get our hands on some again, which isn't easy. Just having the ring alone isn't much of a deterrent. We can't let anyone know I have it, and it only works on one person at a time."

Kaitlyn nodded, eyes searching my face as though in thought. Her hands fluttered to her mouth, hiding it for a moment, then dropped away again. Her whole body tensed, and she backed out of my arms. "Does the ring work on humans too? How many times did you use that thing?"

I frowned, worried by the way she looked at me. "I took many lives when I was a vampire, you know—"

"You weren't a vampire when Harvey died. Was that you?"

Harvey Hall. Her old agent. The man who'd sent her into a vampire LARP game, knowing the girls he sent there sometimes didn't come back. A man who I knew had sent girls off to far worse fates for the right price. I had decided his fate, and I couldn't look away from Kaitlyn's accusing stare, couldn't lie to her. I just nodded.

Her hand flew out and smacked into the wall beside us, but the expression on her face said it was me she wanted to slap. "I feel like I don't even know you."

The door opened and Lance, Bertha, and Niamh strode into the room. "Owen?"

Kaitlyn went silent, but she shot me a look that said our conversation wasn't over.

Bertha marched straight up to me, her gold and blue mask pushed up to her hairline, and her matching gown rustling with every step. "Adelle St Delaurents," she announced, startling Kaitlyn and me to attention. "You told the truth when you said she had died? That she could not have been hiding, or tricking you all this time, secretly alive? Or were you hiding her?"

I stuttered, unsure what to say that wasn't sealing my own fate, unsure what Bertha knew or where her line of questioning came from. "I am sure she was dead."

"She's not anymore. I saw her just now, undead and well."

And there was the proof. Bertha would recognize Adelle. She had known her, because she already ruled on the Synedrion during the short time Adelle and I lived in Umbravallis. Adelle and Bertha were even close, briefly, while Adelle tried to weasel her way into power before deciding the laws of the Synedrion didn't suit her darker tastes.

And now Bertha had seen Adelle. And I had to hope that was all she'd done.

"I saw her too," Kaitlyn said. "She threatened Owen and me."

"And you didn't tell anybody? If she's truly been restored from dust, that has implications. Big ones." Bertha tsked like a much older woman than she appeared to be. "Did you see Dante with her?"

Kaitlyn's eyes were wide. "Can you read minds?"

"No, I can just confirm suspicions. That fool-born varlot!" She muttered a few more unflattering words, then clicked her fingers at the nearby Ebonguard. She shot out orders, and two disappeared from the room. Joss and Heim moved to stand so close to Kaitlyn and me that their shoulders pressed against ours.

"What has Dante got to do with this?" Lance asked. "Not that I don't agree with your description of him, with respect to his position, of course."

Bertha lifted a hand and said nothing. The door swung open again and the rest of the Synedrion members flooded into the room. Even Viatrix. But not Dante.

"Is it true?" Milton demanded. "Has a vampire been raised from the dust?"

"Yes, and one who has a grudge against our humans here, to boot," Bertha confirmed.

The six powerful vampires glanced between themselves. Toren shook his head. "Dante's doing, no doubt."

Shirina swept her arm out, jingling the small bells sewn into her gown. "Why else would he not be here with us now? He also has a history with the risen vampire, Adelle St Delaurents."

"They must be found at once."

Bertha nodded. "I've already sent Ebonguard to rally more and hunt for them."

I was torn. If they were found, Adelle would surely tell the Synedrion what I did with Tiamat's ring. If they didn't find them, Kaitlyn and I would have two more very powerful enemies out there. I looked away, not willing to let any of them see the conflict in my expression.

Lin came toward Kaitlyn. "You two must be protected at all costs."

Does she mean me and Kaitlyn, or Kaitlyn and the child? I didn't know, but relief filled me. As long as they were intent on protecting Kaitlyn, that was all that mattered.

"The Remortalis development is so close," Lin added, frustration clear in her voice. "And we're dealing with grudges and spurned lovers! Why would Dante do something so foolish? He and Adelle must be captured and contained."

Bertha said, "He raised Adelle from the dust, against all orders, knowing he was condemning himself. He must have some sort of plan."

They gave each other grim looks. Shirina pointed to Lance. "Take your humans home. We will double their guard. I'm sure we'll have the criminals captured soon."

Lance nodded, and then we were on the move.

Kaitlyn and I jostled against each other, pressed in from each side by our bodyguards as we made our way out to a waiting car. Joss helped push Kaitlyn, and her pile of skirts and hoops, in through the door, and Bertha joined us on the trip.

As we sped through Umbravallis, she grilled me on everything related to Adelle. Where she might have gone. Any acquaintances they could seek shelter with. Why she and Dante had such a grudge against me.

As I hesitated over my answers, Kaitlyn spoke up, saving me, "Why is this even happening now? How could Dante bring her back?"

Bertha sighed, a motion of her chest which exhaled no air. "You returned Kissare's chalice to us."

"This is *my* fault now?" Kaitlyn's fury was palpable. "Oh, sorry I got kidnapped by an eating disorder cult for vampires who happened to have one of your precious vampire artifacts. My bad."

Bertha smacked her lips. "You done? Of course it's not your fault. It's a simple case that your misfortune was our good fortune. And fortune indeed, because that is the power of Kissare's chalice. I speak of the timing, that once the chalice returned to us, we were able to see in it the function of Ri's flute and Damkina's veil."

I whistled softly. That was big news. The veil and flute had been in the possession of the Synedrion for centuries, but never in our history had anyone discovered their powers. Some believed they had none and debated whether they were even true artifacts of the seven. This proved that they were. "They bring vampires back from true-death? How?"

"I obviously can't share that information with you."

"They have to be used together," Kaitlyn whispered.

"How could you know that?" Bertha snapped.

"Just from what you said, and what I read of vampire history in the book Lance got me. You said 'the function,' singular, of the *two* items. And Ri and Damkina, their love story, their tragic end, their vow to return to each other even after death? I mean, it's obvious."

Bertha's voice turned cold. "Only the members of the Synedrion possessed the knowledge that such a revival could even occur. We agreed, all of us, that it wasn't to be used, and was to be kept secret. Dante only agreed begrudgingly."

"This better not be a 'now you know we have to kill you' moment," Kaitlyn muttered.

"The important point to note is that in order to revive the dead vampire, you must have their remains. Dante must have kept some of Adelle's ashes all these years, and if he had her ashes, it may have been true after all that he was there when she died, or soon after." Bertha directed this all at me, her eyes narrowed. I couldn't say anything in return.

Kaitlyn saved me again. "Does that include your

gruesome statue collection? The ones turned to stone with What's-His-Name's dagger?"

"Potentially. But that is the danger of this knowledge and power. The potential."

We all grew silent then, dwelling on that potential. We already stood at the doorway to a whole new world, one where vampires could become human again, or wouldn't be reliant on human blood, and now there was the power to truly have vampires live forever, no matter what. It was clear from the silence that all of us thought that was too much power. But some would demand that power be used. Among those turned to stone by Alam's dagger were two of the original seven themselves.

We arrived at Lance's just as Bertha received the news that Dante and Adelle were nowhere to be found. Dawn was coming, and Bertha left us so she could oversee the continuing hunt.

Once back inside, the Ebonguard gave us some space again, and Kaitlyn and I headed straight for bed. She refused help getting out of her monstrosity of a gown and into her pajamas. When she lay down beside me, she was stiff as a board and silent.

I stared at her, unable to say all the things I wanted to say, only being able to mutter, "I need to make sure you are safe."

I rolled over to face her but she wouldn't look at me, just lay there staring up at the splashes of early morning sunlight on the ceiling. "If I was a vampire …"

She launched herself from the bed. Her lips curled back in disgust. "You'd kill me. Or feed from me. Also, the baby. Would you feed from this baby too?"

Her words, so cold I could feel the chill in the air between us, sent me toward her. But when I tried to get close to her, she backed away.

"I would never."

"No. No, you wouldn't, and do you know why? Because I won't ever be your captive again. Never. I won't stay with you if you become a vampire. You would never be able to protect me as a vampire because I would have nothing to do with you."

She stormed out the door and slammed it so hard behind her the room shook. I slumped onto the side of the bed, groaning with frustration. A few minutes passed. She didn't return.

And just being away from her, those moments when she was out of my sight and I missed her and feared for her and wanted her, told me everything I needed to know. That I couldn't protect her as a vampire. That all I could do, and what I *had* to do, was just be there for her. To love her, and be better for her as I was. As a human. Because that was who she loved.

I muttered a few swear words, then headed out the door.

Lance was in the hallway. Joss guarded one end and Heim guarded the other.

"Kaitlyn?" I asked him.

He pointed his chin at another room. "I wouldn't. It's locked."

"You heard all that?"

"I was just looking for Dusky. But you weren't exactly being quiet." He looked me up and down. "You looking to rejoin us?"

"Are you offering? You refused me before."

He shrugged. "I had a bad case of the feelings at the time. But you're like my brother, or once were. I owe you many times over. You ask a favor of me, I will help you."

Immortality. Strength. Power. All right there for the taking. And all it would cost me was Kaitlyn.

"No. I don't want that. Not anymore." I leaned heavily against the wall. Tears sprung into my eyes and hung there, the truth stinging my heart and making it grow full. "But there is something you can help me with. I have to go and get something from the castle in Slovakia."

Lance lifted an eyebrow. "You need it now? I said ask a favor, but that is pushing it, considering everything going on."

"Yes. I need it now. And it has to be in secret."

"What could be so important?"

"A ring. For Kaitlyn."

A huge grin grew on Lance's face. He touched a hand to his chest as though surprised. "How about that? I guess my case of the feelings is still hanging around after all."

11

KAITLYN

I sat cross-legged on the bed in one of the many unoccupied bedrooms. The only light came from the glow of my phone screen as I scrolled down through all the missed calls and messages. We'd been allowed to keep our phones this time, but something had been done to them so they only received incoming messages. Nothing outgoing, no internet.

Just enough so I could sit here and read all the angry messages from my agent and PR company, demanding to know where I was. Why wasn't I answering my phone? Why hadn't I made it to that entertainment magazine interview? Was I in rehab? Was I going to make it to that premiere? Tonight?

No. I didn't think I was going to make it. And I couldn't even let them know why.

I was so sick of my life not being *mine*. I'd been held captive for too long, trading one prison for another, one horror for another, and I was done with it.

Hot tears pricked my eyelids. All I'd ever wanted, since I was a child, was to be an actor. I'd gone to LA as a fresh-faced small-town girl determined to make it. I'd taken every crappy walk-on bit part I could. I'd studied my craft. I'd worked as a low-paid extra. I'd stood in cattle-call lines for sometimes twelve hours at a stretch just to be told that they'd already cast that part.

I'd been so desperate I'd agreed to play a victim to vampires in a LARP game that turned out to be way too real. And I was *still* playing victim to those vampires. They weren't drinking my blood, but they were still taking my life.

I kept thinking about a script I'd looked at last month. The heroine was a badass, fighting her way out of anything, with martial arts and perfect hair. I'd thought I could take on that role, had even started training for it, because I had faith that I was a good enough actress to do anything. I wished reality was like that—that I could just step into the role I needed to play and deliver the perfect one-liners as I kicked vampire butt and saved myself and those I loved.

I knew too well that that wasn't reality. I'd still fight, tooth and claw and matted hair. But I was just an actress and would never be strong enough compared to a vampire.

Maybe Owen was right.

I whimpered. Right or wrong, he was trying to find a solution, and we were in this together. Sulking and shutting him out wouldn't get us anywhere.

I unlocked the door and stepped into the hallway. Heim stood at the end of the hall, guarding. Joss was gone, which could only mean Owen was gone too. Now she was on 'secondary' duty; she shadowed him just as Heim shadowed me.

I snarled as I walked past him into the living area. I wished he'd do that Ebonguard invisible-to-humans trick like they had on the plane, so I could stop seeing his dumb face, even what little I could see of it. Sure, he was doing his job, protecting me, but that protection came at the cost of my freedom. At that point, I'd rather be free.

Lance paced in the kitchen, running a hand along the granite counter, back and forth. "Night's greetings," he said, distracted.

"Owen's gone somewhere?"

Lance glanced at me and shrugged.

"Do you know where he is?"

"He'll be back soon." Under his breath he added, "Better be."

"So you do know where he is."

He paused in his pacing, grimacing as though caught out. "Maybe."

I walked over to the lounge and flopped onto it, too tired for vampire riddles. I patted the seat next to me.

Lance shook his head. "Shouldn't. I haven't eaten, and you're smelling remarkably delicious. Have you seen Dusky?"

Oh. Dusky. Shit. "I think we left her behind. At the ball. After all the commotion."

Lance grunted, his fangs showing, and came over to dump himself down in an armchair across from me. I tried to be subtle as I measured with my eyes the distance between him and me, and Heim and me, just in case an intervention was needed.

"She should still be back by now."

"Maybe she decided to stay and have fun for a bit longer, since we totally abandoned the poor human girl there." I leaned into the words, trying to get Lance to see what dicks we'd been.

Lance waved my tone away. "She'll be fine. Everyone knows she belongs to me."

I raised an eyebrow. "Will Owen be fine? Where is he?"

"Joss is with him."

"That wasn't an answer to my question. Why are you being so secretive?"

"Because he asked me to? Because you two aren't meant to be going anywhere? Because sorting out his little excursion to Slovakia could get us all in trouble?" Lance lifted his hands, clearly at a loss.

Deathless

I tapped my fingers on the arm of the sofa. "Slovakia?"

Lance grimaced again. "This is unfair, interrogating me when I'm hungry and *distracted*." I didn't miss how his fangs sat over his lips and his eyes stared at my neckline.

But all that mattered at the moment was that Owen was gone. And he hadn't even said goodbye. He'd found a way to be gone, a way maybe we could have escaped, but he hadn't taken me. I took a long, calming breath. No, he could have only convinced Lance to help him get out if he'd promised to be right back. Just a quick trip. To get something. There could only be one thing he'd risk that for.

I lowered my voice, turning my head away from the watching Ebonguard. "Did he say he was going to get something? A ring, maybe?"

Lance looked shocked. "You already know?"

"Yeah. I'm surprised that you do."

"He just told me when he asked to go." Lance tutted. "It was meant to be a surprise."

I eyed him. He was taking the whole cursed-forbidden-ring thing very lightly.

Maybe I was the one overreacting. Maybe this was all everyday shenanigans in vampire world.

I sighed, slumping back into the lounge, trying to let it absorb me. "Maybe we do need a weapon after all."

Lance leaned forward, eyebrows raised. "Sorry,

what? How did we get to weapons?"

"Just, you know. We need a way to protect ourselves. We're no match for vampires as we are."

"I can't make the offer of change to you as well, sorry," Lance said. "The Synedrion want to keep their precious blood-sample human. Not to mention your condition." He pointed to my belly.

Part of me hated the idea of becoming a vampire, but part of me had become desperate. "It would mean losing the child, wouldn't it? Becoming a vampire."

Lance nodded. I wasn't that desperate.

"Maybe it wouldn't be so terrible if Owen was a vampire again. Maybe he could feed from me just enough to keep his human empathy, but not enough to be human. Maybe he could keep us safe. He would be able to fight other vampires if he was one." And maybe after everything was over, he could change into a human again.

But it might never be over. That might become our unhappily ever after, being fed on and protected by a being I would grow to despise.

Vampires had no empathy. They could have loving relationships, but not as we humans understood love. They didn't have the emotional toolkit for that complex stew of emotions. Their love was cold, unflinching, a power play of greed and want and lust, geared toward whatever suited them, and not the other person in the relationship.

I couldn't let him do that. He wouldn't be *Owen*. He wouldn't be the man I loved.

"I don't think it would be terrible. Mortality, that sounds terrible," Lance scoffed.

"But wait, you said make the offer to me *as well*? Did you offer to turn Owen?"

Lance shrugged as though it was nothing. "He turned me down."

"He did?" My heart jumped to a gallop.

"You seem surprised. Or is it disappointed?"

"No, not disappointed." Proud. Warmed through with love. Burning with the happiness of getting to keep Owen tinged with the fear of losing everything.

That was why he went to get the ring. He needed something, some way of offering protection that didn't come at the cost of losing *us*. A token to prove we did still have options.

Maybe there were other options we hadn't looked at enough. Like if only we could get away, we could switch sides and get help from the vampire hunters. With the tech they had, surely they had an R&D department that could weaponize the cure from my blood. Free the world from vampires forever.

But as long as even one vampire remained, they could turn more. And with the veil and flute trick they'd discovered now, even actual death wasn't permanent to them anymore. I had to accept vampires were a thing and they weren't going anywhere.

I grumbled, "Are there any magic wands out there that make people immune to vampires?"

"Sure," Lance said. "Check down the back of the couch. I think I lost one down there with some pocket change."

"Don't be crabby at me because you're hungry. I was serious. Kind of."

"No. Well, maybe. I mean, magical objects aren't exactly common. The only known items of power are those cursed with the spirits of the original seven. And of those, we know Alam's dagger, Kissare's chalice, Tiamat's ring, Ri's flute, and Damkina's veil. We have no idea what Dagan's item even is."

I counted off the names on my fingers. "That's six. What about the seventh? What was his name again? Mordak?"

"Marduk. He was the very last of the seven to die. He was the one who wrote many of our laws. Many of the cruelest laws as well, and also put them into practice. It was him who built the Sun Shrine. Those who knew him say he was benevolent at first, but insanity took over toward the end, and he took a bit too much joy in delivering punishments."

"So, a vampire who enjoyed burning other vampires alive for days? Okay, I can't wait to find out what his object does." I hid my interest under sarcasm.

"You and all of vampirekind. It is also unknown, undiscovered." Lance leaned forward, as though telling a spooky campfire story. "But there have always been rumors that it was something devastating to vampires, that it has remained hidden because no one desires to be near something so awful."

"A bit like me, huh?" A high-pitched voice broke the mood. Dusky had walked up behind Lance, looking frazzled with her red hair let out and high heels dangling from one hand.

I winced. "I'm sorry. We had a bit of a situation and had to leave in a hurry."

Dusky's voice raised an octave. "And you all just forgot about me?"

"Not at all," Lance said. "I've been wondering where you were."

"Why? 'Cause you're hungry?"

Lance's fangs were a dead giveaway.

She stamped a bare foot. "I had to walk home!"

She stormed off to her bedroom. Lance tried to follow her in, but the door slammed in his face.

I leveled a look at him. "You've got to end this, Lance."

Lance growled at me, and sped off so fast I could only see a blur.

12

KAITLYN

I wandered around Lance's dusty mansion for some time, waiting and anxious, before I found a small door leading to an even smaller balcony, one with a narrow, steep staircase that led right up onto the roof.

The pitched tiles shifted and crunched under my weight as I climbed up, and I tentatively shuffled over into the valley between two roofs, which made an almost comfortable place to sit.

I could just make out Heim's silhouette against the night sky, watching from a ridge on the lower wing, but I could pretend I was alone.

I sat there while the sky lightened, and swallows darted across the eggshell-blue expanse, chasing clouds of tiny gnats. A low wind made the long grass

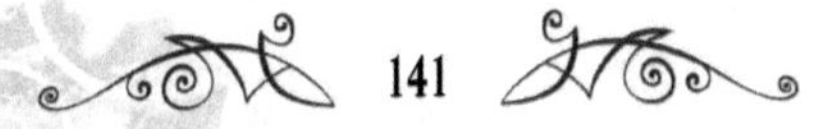

all around the house sway like ocean waves.

The sun appeared, the first thin beam shining straight, like a golden arrow, through the gap between cliffs, right into the Sun Shrine. From up here, the shape of the ancient temple stood out clearly. Megalithic stones met together in two curves, with two more circles of stones inside, almost like an eye. The inner circles were covered, and the whole thing was built down into a sort of amphitheater, carved out of the stony mountainside.

The rumble of a helicopter came from the distance, then a moment later, Joss appeared on the path leading up to the house, carrying Owen. Joss placed Owen back on his feet, then she looked directly up at me. I felt almost like I'd been caught out, but I wasn't the one doing something wrong. How did she spot me so fast? She probably smelled my blood.

It wasn't long before Owen came up and joined me on the roof.

"Night's greetings," he said. *The greeting of a vampire.*

"It's dawn."

He turned to look at the sky, as though verifying what I'd said. "You look tired."

"My days and nights are already getting mixed up." A tear crept down my face.

He moved forward, catching it with his finger.

"You have a nice trip?" I didn't mean to be catty,

but it slipped out.

He sighed and sat beside me. "It was meant to be a secret."

"I can't believe you managed to escape, even for a while, and you didn't take me."

"I didn't escape. Joss was with me the whole time." He thumb-pointed behind us where Joss had joined Heim on the other ridge, like two gargoyles, their eyes and faces completely masked from the rising sun.

"You know what I mean. How did you do it?"

"Lance can be persuasive. Joss was still technically fulfilling her duty, guarding me. She's the only one who knows how far away we actually went. And I promised to be back by morning." He sucked in a breath. "I'm sorry I went without you, but I had to—"

"I know why you went." And I understood. But a night of overthinking had left my emotions ragged. A sob squeaked out.

I wanted the freedom Owen had just had, even if only for a few hours. I wanted my life back. It was *mine* but it kept being stolen from me. First by Vampire Owen, then the Starved, and now the Synedrion. I wanted to be forever free of the vampires, to be free of this. I couldn't even think past the need to *go*, the need to have my own life again.

Owen tried to pull me close, but I resisted. I couldn't let him hold me, because if I did, I would forget how awful everything was, just how badly I needed to be free.

The sun had risen high enough to touch us with its light, and I yawned. I was tired of living a life flipped upside down. I should have been waking up, not ready for bed. I should have been on a beach or sitting at a table drinking coffee and reading scripts, or preparing for my premiere, or … or shopping for baby clothes and nursery furniture.

All the normal things people did.

Owen relaxed onto the tiles, lying on his back, and staring at the few puffs of cloud floating above us. "I'm sorry for using the ring on your agent. I'd created this whole story of a ring that sought out those who deserved it. And I *knew* Harvey deserved it. I think we both did."

I nodded, propped up on my elbows beside him, heart heavy.

"My thinking was messed up, but I just didn't want to leave you thinking that he *didn't* deserve it—that if such a thing existed out there, that could deliver righteous vengeance for us, I didn't want to leave you questioning why you had no vengeance for his crimes."

My tears dried up, and I sniffled away the remains of them. "But that's the thing. I never really wanted vengeance. Justice, maybe. Or knowing that he wasn't sending other girls to terrible fates—that would be good too. But not *vengeance*. It's not a thing I generally seek out. That's what monsters do, what vampires do."

"And I'm sorry I made you think that was what I wanted to be again. I don't want that. Not anymore."

"I know. Lance told me you turned him down." I reached out and squeezed Owen's fingers.

"There's more though." Owen turned onto his side, staring into my eyes, his own the color of the sky around us. "I know now that just becoming human isn't enough. I have to actually work hard to be a *good* human. And I promise you I will. For you, for me, and for our child."

I turned onto my side as well, pressing my body to his, my forehead to his, nose to his. "I love you," I said, at the same time hushed and bursting with passion.

I smothered his reply, feeling the word love on his lips as I met them with mine. The kiss was long and lingering, countless smaller kisses flowing together into one.

A big yawn cracked my mouth open, and I stared at the full morning sunshine for a moment.

Owen nuzzled a kiss into my hairline. "You need sleep."

"I wish. I have to go be a good little lab rat for Shirina and Lin, remember?" My mouth folded downward.

"Tell them to wait. Tell them no."

"Ha," I barked it loud enough that the Ebonguard

turned their heads our way. "No, you know that isn't going to work. Besides, it sounds like they're also pulling all-dayers to try to get their cure finished. You can smell the obsession on the air."

The word obsession made Owen frown, and my first thought went to Adelle. A thought that felt too close to jealousy. I swatted it away, because Owen chose me. He chose me over becoming a vampire again. He'd always choose me. As long as we survived.

"Owen, if ..." I drew closer to him. I put my mouth to his ear and dropped my voice. "If they find out what happened with Adelle, what will they do?"

His gaze went straight to the Sun Shrine. My heart sunk all the way to my stomach.

"Then we have to fight fire with fire. Or with whatever we can get." I nodded toward the shrine as well. "Lance was telling me about the guy who built that place, that his relic still hasn't been found, but is probably something powerful. *Devastating*, he said. If we could find it, if we could work it out, it could be like our nuclear deterrent."

"That's a lot of ifs," Owen said.

"I know. I know I'm basically daydreaming, but I need some hope to keep me going. That other thing you have, well, I know it's only good for one-at-a-time stuff, and I think it's probably best kept hidden to avoid trouble, yeah?" I gave Owen a pointed look, hoping he understood. "But something *devastating*, well, we could be flashy with that, because who would come after us if we had it?"

Owen smiled, his eyes thoughtful. "It's a good plan." He kissed me between my eyebrows. "Come on then, let's get off this roof. I'll stay up as well, so I'll be awake when you return."

I took his hand and he helped me to my feet. "It's okay. You can sleep."

He shook his head and kissed my nose. "I have something for you, for when you get back."

I tilted my head, curious. What could he mean? Owen loved treating me with gifts, but surprise presents seemed out of place with the situation we were in now. Maybe he was just trying to keep things feeling normal. Keep being the man I loved.

I wanted to pretend things were normal too. I couldn't believe I was suggesting we find a mysterious magical relic, one with devastating powers. Fighting and killing weren't what I wanted.

But as I followed Owen down off that rooftop, saying goodbye to the sunlight and stepping back into the shadows again, I knew I was going to have to fight to be free.

I had to stop thinking like a victim and start thinking like a predator.

13

OWEN

I meant every word I said to Kaitlyn. I wanted to be a good person, a better man for her. But I also still wanted to protect her.

Not as a vampire. Not anymore. But somehow.

What she mentioned about Marduk and the Sun Shrine got me thinking. It was true his relic had never been found, but there had been plenty of rumors about it over the centuries. It may have been an impossible hope, but I had managed to find one of the seven's possessions before. Maybe I could find one again.

In the past, I'd had the time, resources, and freedom of a wealthy vampire. Now, I'd just have to make do with what I had. And it *had* to be enough. This body, this life. It was enough.

Straight after I'd showered, I convinced Joss to take me to the Synedrion estate. After all, it should be one of the safer places in Umbravallis. With Kaitlyn off in the lab with Lin and Shirina, guarded by Heim, Joss seemed antsy herself. I would have preferred if Joss was still Kaitlyn's primary bodyguard too.

A car took us to the estate, and we entered a long, low building, off to the side of the main palace. I had no idea where to start looking, but Umbravallis's archives seemed like a good choice. Maybe I could see the old stories in a new light. Kaitlyn had so easily understood the use of the flute and veil based on Ri and Damkina's relationship. Maybe looking with human eyes, with that bit of extra emotion, could give me a clue that a vampire wouldn't see.

I walked up the smooth marble steps and pushed the heavy wooden door open. The floor was cold below my shoes—the chill drifted up through the soles and the thin protection of my dress socks, and I found myself longing for the ranch, for the sunshine, and smell of horses and orange trees blossoming. For hot wind blowing dry dust across the day. I knew Kaitlyn longed for that sunshine, that freedom, just as much as I did if not more.

We had to be on the offensive now. Not just to save our freedom, but to save our lives.

I knew the time that Kaitlyn's life was protected

was limited. As soon as they'd perfected their synthetic blood and vampirism cure from her actual blood, the Synedrion wouldn't need her anymore. What would happen to Kaitlyn when she was no longer necessary? When it wasn't worth protecting her, but the risk of letting her go was too great?

The archive entryway was lined with statues, just as the entryway into the Synedrion's chambers were. Not really statues, though. I stared at the face of the woman in front of me, her flesh turned to stone by Alam's dagger. I wondered what her crime had been, to deserve this punishment. Or if *any* crime deserved this punishment.

That the ones I once called friends were cruel enough to turn living, thinking beings to stone, and then display them in such a manner, wasn't something I had thought much about before. But now, standing here, I wondered if there was still a working mind inside that stone prison. If there was hunger and thirst. If there was pain and sorrow.

And if I might be the next statue in that terrible display.

An archivist nodded silently to me as I walked down the aisles. Tall shelving of carved dark wood and leather-bound tomes ran the length of each room, with gaps here and there filled with armchairs and study desks, each room joining another similar space. I breathed in the earthy smell of the books and headed for the section housing titles on the original seven. I'd only have access to the basic, public area, despite knowing that underground were floors and floors of archives, only accessible with permits. But I couldn't ask for one without a good reason.

A lot of the information in the archives had been digitized, but Kaitlyn and I weren't currently allowed online, and the digital collection of history texts were exclusively accessible by vampires, so my access had probably been revoked.

I would simply have to look and read the old-fashioned way to try to find a magical object that had remained unknown for more than a millennium.

I continued toward the back of the archives. Each room was colder than the last, and the aisles of books seemed to go on forever. The place was pin-drop quiet, and my footsteps echoed.

Through the final doorway at the very end of the building was a treasure trove of ancient books. Glass cases displayed the oldest documents, opened to whatever the archivists deemed the most interesting or visually beautiful page, and the whole room was temperature-controlled to preserve those books for as long as possible.

Joss walked in beside me, covered by the usual uniform and armor. Would that armor be much protection against whatever devastating effect Marduk's relic held? I shouldn't care. I had to keep reminding myself she was the enemy.

Thankfully, once we reached the final room, she stationed herself at the door and let me be. The last thing I needed was for her to work out what I was looking for.

But even I wasn't sure exactly what I was seeking. I started with the shelved books, picking relevant titles and flicking through them until my eyes grew weary and blurred. I rubbed them, sighed, then turned my attention to the glass table-top cabinets. I leaned over the protective cases, peering down at the illuminated pages and ragged papyrus scrolls on display. The first showed an illustration of Tiamat burning at the stake, a medieval representation of an event that had occurred nearly three thousand years ago. Another had a portrait, executed in angular and stilted Babylonian-style brushwork, of Ri playing her flute, as Damkina sat with her jealous husband, Kissare. I skimmed along, looking for anything on Marduk, and finally found a selection of loose pages with silverpoint sketches, showing the Sun Shrine. The largest sketch depicted a carving from within the Sun Shrine of the face of Marduk. His single eye stared up at me.

"Owen?" Bertha's voice made me flinch.

"What are you doing up in daylight hours?" I turned around, trying to pretend I hadn't been caught off guard and wasn't interested in what I'd just been looking at.

She made a face at my informal greeting, but seemed to shrug it off. "Wandering. Thinking. Waiting for news."

"And has there been any?"

"Nothing yet. No sign of Dante and Adelle." She walked over and peered down into the tabletop display I had been studying.

"How hard are you looking?" I asked.

"Hard enough. They took Ri's flute and Damkina's veil with them when they left. They must be recovered before any more damage is done."

"More damage?"

Bertha sighed. "A statue is missing."

I didn't know what to say to that. I stood silent, wondering why Bertha was being so free with information with us lately. As though our existence was already deemed so temporary it hardly mattered. "Which statue?"

Her lips pursed and she shook her head. Whether she was unwilling to admit it due to the gravity of the theft, or my knowing was not allowed after all, I wasn't sure.

She stared at the silverpoint sketches, then with a perfectly manicured red nail, tapped the glass directly over the image of Marduk, the carving of his face with only one eye.

"I'd forgotten about that carving; it's been so long

since I've seen it. It's been covered in ash for centuries."

I shuddered. The ash of all those who'd been bound to the sun. Their ashes were left where they burned, and since their bodies regenerated each night and burned each day, sometimes for weeks, a lot of ash had accumulated over the centuries. As the Sun Shrine and the rituals there were considered sacred, that ash was never cleared away.

She tsked. "One eye? That doesn't seem right."

I looked again, but couldn't see anything out of place. Marduk was famous for only having one eye. He'd lost one when he was still human. Trying to become whole again was part of the driving force for why he and the others became the first seven. But becoming a vampire, gaining immortality, hadn't helped him regrow that eye.

She leaned in closer, and I saw her squinting at the fine print scribbled below the sketch. "Of course, this was drawn a long time after the shrine was constructed and filled with ash. The artist probably drew it based on assumptions or false information. I feel though that I remember the carving in the temple showing Marduk with two eyes. The story was he commissioned it to show himself as he'd always wished to be."

No other depiction of Marduk showed him with two eyes. He was always shown with one, even when he'd commissioned the works. At least to my knowledge. And some distant memory told me the carving in the temple was only completed after Marduk's death.

I looked again with human eyes, imagining Marduk's longing to be whole. Many of the other cursed relics or their powers in some way symbolized a yearning of its owner. Kissare wished for visions to prove his wife's infidelity. Tiamat swore death and vengeance as she was burned. Ri and Damkina wished to save each other, in that life and forever afterwards. And Marduk and his eyes ...

This... this could be something.

But my memory and knowledge were nothing compared to Bertha's.

"You knew them, didn't you? Marduk and Damkina?"

Bertha turned away from the drawing, leaning her slim teenage figure against the case and folding her arms. "I only knew Damkina for a short time. I was one of the last of her many children. Marduk, I knew for longer, but I missed knowing him in his days of greatness. I only knew him when his insanity had taken hold."

To have known the original seven, to have walked the earth at the same time as two of them, was awe-inspiring. "I often forget how old you are."

Bertha's head dipped, and she looked tired. "Me too."

"You're sure it has two eyes? The carving in the shrine?" I tried not to sound too interested.

Bertha's expression had become distant and she wandered away. "No. I'm not sure. It was too many lifetimes ago."

She said her goodbye as she passed Joss at the doorway, a quiet, sad goodbye, and I waited a moment longer before taking my phone out to take a picture of the sketch. I found an empty office on the way out and ran off a copy of the photo. I folded the thin paper and pocketed it, still warm from the printer.

I stepped out of the archives and the cold air slapped against me, a fresh wind that awakened my spirit. I felt alive, and hopeful, and eager to share my discovery with Kaitlyn.

Joss and I returned to Lance's, and since Kaitlyn wasn't back yet, I went straight to find the ring box I had buried in a jar of rice in the kitchen. Joss watched from the corner, but it didn't matter if she saw it. She'd already seen me collect it when she took me to the castle in Slovakia.

I grabbed a pen and marked up the copy of the sketch, folded it small, tucked it inside the ring box, then placed them on the counter. And then I paced, waiting, eager, and excited.

Footsteps dashed up the stairs and I turned to them, only to be met by Dusky. Her face was twisted in fear.

"It's Kaitlyn! Quick. Kaitlyn's in trouble and needs help!"

Ice shot through my nerves, and I turned straight to Joss. She was already halfway out of the room, but paused, and looked back at me.

"No, go. Go fast. Don't worry about me—just get to Kaitlyn. I'll be right behind you."

Joss gave a single nod, then disappeared in a black blur.

Kaitlyn's in trouble. What trouble? It didn't matter. I only hoped Joss was fast enough. I knew I was slower, too slow, but I couldn't help anyway. I only had one thing powerful enough to even possibly help, and I had to get it.

I rushed into our bedroom, tearing off the covers and reaching my hand into the gash I'd cut in the side of the mattress. My fingers closed on the small book and pulled it out. Adelle's diary.

I opened the petite journal, and stared down at Tiamet's ring, nestled in the pages. I'd cut out large hunks of Adelle's handwritten words and placed the ring that killed her within them. It felt right and wrong all at the same time, but it worked as a hiding place for forbidden treasure.

I dashed back to the living area to find Dusky lounging there casually.

"She really has become obsessed with Kaitlyn, hasn't she?" she said.

"Who?" My first thought was Adelle. That Adelle had gone after Kaitlyn.

Deathless

Dusky laughed. "Joss, silly. She didn't even stop to think of your safety, which, you know, is her job. She just ran to save precious Kaitlyn."

I stood there, Adelle's diary in my hand, staring at Dusky in horror as more footsteps pounded up the stairs. A dozen human thralls poured into the room.

Headed straight for me.

14

KAITLYN

The lab was crisply lit, and the smell of the alcohol wipe Lin pressed against my arm was extra strong.

"Everything seems to be progressing normally with your pregnancy," Lin told me. She'd run a few tests since I was there, including a quick ultrasound. I had a little printout of the scan in my hand, although it was barely more than a grainy gray background with a grainy gray dot. I also held a couple of printouts from the internet she'd found for me on early pregnancy care, since I hadn't had a chance to look into it myself. I knew the basic stuff, like no alcohol, but no soft cheeses? For nine months? Were they kidding me?

"Thank you," I said, and meant it. Lin was one of the few vampires who still treated me somewhat like

a human. Shirina wasn't bad either, but she still looked at me more like a specimen than a sentient being. She had kept herself busy on the cure project, which she'd dubbed Remortalis, running some high-tech process on the blood sample I'd given when I first came in.

I was almost ready to leave when she requested just a bit more. She seemed excited, like she'd made some kind of breakthrough. "Two vials, please," she called from the back corner. "This is very promising. Very."

I looked away as Lin clicked the vacuum tubes on and off. I could never watch as they drew blood, or gave me injections, which seemed to come in equal measure for one reason or another. I pretended not to notice as she licked her lips. "Be sure to rehydrate. Next time, try to hydrate yourself more before having blood drawn too."

Next time. My inner voice was super petulant. It even blew a raspberry. I smiled politely as I applied pressure to the needle hole with a cotton ball.

Lin handed the vials to Heim, who was standing guard by my side, and shooed him off. He didn't appear to be happy being used to ferry my blood samples across the room to Shirina, but he did it anyway. Lin went to find a plaster for my arm.

The glass door banged against the wall, clattering as Joss appeared like a black flash in front of me.

"Kaitlyn! Are you—?" She broke off, looking at

me, then the room, assessing everything.

I gawked at her.

Heim returned, looking around as well. "Why are you here? Where is your human charge?"

Joss's eyes were wide. "Dusky just told us that you were in trouble. That I had to come and help."

"I'm fine. No trouble." Trepidation wormed itself into my belly. Prickles shot along the base of my spine and lodged into my hairline. "Wait. Why would Dusky tell you that?"

Joss's head shook, but she had no answer.

My voice came out thin and highly pitched. "Where's Owen?"

I didn't even wait for an answer. I took off at a dead run. Hands closed around my waist and I cried out, expecting to be pulled back. But the hands lifted me and I was being carried in Joss's arms, since she was able to run so much faster than I ever could.

The shadowed town passed by us in flashes, our path as straight as an arrow with no garden or wall or building standing as obstacle to Joss's momentum. She cradled me easily as she leaped and dashed through the quiet daytime streets, empty even though the sunlight didn't reach into the dark valley. Then we were on the road up the hill, through the long grass, and up the stairs into Lance's top-floor human habitat.

Sunlight flooded in and Joss dropped me, gasping

and shielding her uncovered eyes with her arm.

I was vaguely aware of her finding the remote and closing the curtains, but all I could see was the chaos before me. All I could hear was the scream echoing in my brain.

Owen!

"OWEN?" I called out into the space but knew there would be no answer.

The living area had been trashed. Rugs were kicked up and humped over in weird shapes. A side table had been smashed. The cushions from the lounge were all over the place, stuffing ripped and torn.

Joss bent down to sniff something. Blood.

When she slammed her fist into the floor so hard I felt the house shake, I knew whose blood it had to be.

No, he can't be gone. Horror flooded through me. He'd been taken, taken from me. And I was pretty sure who took him. And that Dusky, vamp fangirl extraordinaire, had helped them.

It didn't take a genius to figure that out. There was more blood near the kitchen and … I blinked at the tiny box on the counter. A ring box. *Oh no.*

I dashed over to grab it, hoping Joss didn't notice.

Dread coiled like a boa constrictor around my stomach. In this box was the cursed ring, Tiamat's ring. I didn't want to look at it, to see it. But I had to check that it was still in there.

The box snapped open on its spring, and the ring

inside was … gorgeous. Pale rose-gold filigree and a large, clear diamond that sparked rainbows in every facet. No blood drop-shaped ruby. No tarnished silver. I inhaled a shaky gasp.

Joss stood by me, looking at the ring as well.

"Was this the ring he went to get?" My heart pounded, sounding in my ears like a grieving bell.

"That's what he went to Slovakia for. A big risk when he could have proposed with something else," Joss said softly.

I felt tears spilling from my eyes. "He didn't get anything else?"

"Just that ring and a small book."

I touched the ring softly with one finger, wishing I could be touching Owen's cheek. I noticed a piece of folded paper wedged up into the top of the ring box.

Joss crumpled, dropping onto her knees. "I have failed."

Heim appeared, followed by two other Ebonguard he must have collected on the way. "Where is he?"

Joss was back at attention before I could blink through my tears to see clearly. I slipped the ring onto my finger and quickly pocketed the box.

"Gone," Joss reported.

His hand shot out, and Joss went flying across the room. Her back hit the wall and she crashed to the floor.

An indignant scream broke from my lips. "What

the fuck is wrong with you?"

He pushed me out of his way so easily I might as well have been made of the lightest straw. "Be quiet," he ordered.

Joss got to her feet, composing herself again into a neat pose of attention. "I'm sorry. I should have known something was wrong. I acted in haste."

"You acted against your commands. You should never have left your charge." Heim's voice was cold, but there was a dark revelry in his words. "You were always the fastest, the most talented, but you never were good with orders. You've just used your third strike."

I tried to step between them. "Dusky tricked her; it's not her fault." I knew just how seriously Joss took her job. She'd jumped out of an airplane for it. "She was just trying to help me, and why are you just standing here being mad at Joss when Owen's been kidnapped, and Dusky and whoever she's working with could still be on the grounds? Go after them!" My voice rose and broke, nails on chalkboard in the quiet tension. But nobody moved.

Heim spoke to Joss in a low, grim voice, "You will be stripped of your rank, take your punishment, and be exiled forever." He stepped forward, and ripped Joss's cowl straight off her, leaving her face exposed. Her dark skin shone hot with fury and shame, lit up with an inside glow as pink as her hair. She remained at attention, her whole body shaking. Her lips were set tight.

"No!" My voice rose in a wail. "I want her as my guard! I need—"

One of the other Ebonguard clapped a hand over my mouth. I bit at his fingers but he didn't even flinch. I sagged against his stone-like body, my thoughts swirling and flying uselessly.

Joss took one long, slow look at me, bared her teeth in a snarl, then pushed Heim out of her face with both hands. He crashed into the opposite wall hard enough to leave a crater.

And then she fled.

"Joss?" I whispered, but she was gone.

Heim picked himself up from the floor. He moved at odd angles and reset broken bones with a crunch until he could stand properly again. Then he glared at me.

"Guard her, and do not leave her side for even one second," he told the remaining Ebonguards.

Then he too was gone, and I was left there, weeping furiously, with my thoughts tangled and my heart breaking into a million shredded bits.

Joss was gone.

Dusky had betrayed us.

Owen had been taken.

And I was helpless to find him, or help Joss, or even help myself.

15

OWEN

My body ached all over, bruised and cut from trying to fight the thralls that had come for me. I'd fought my hardest, but there were just too many of them. I winced as they carried me, bumped and jostled in their zombie-like grasp, slung between them like I was being taken to a cannibal's feast.

They'd bound my wrists and ankles and thrown a bag over my head so I couldn't see where we went, but when they took the bag off, I knew exactly where we were. I'd never forget that place. Even though it had been changed.

They dumped me out onto a stone table, and sickness lurched through me. This was the place the Starved had taken us, the same table they'd bound Kaitlyn to, the place where they'd enthralled me and I'd almost harmed her in a way I could never forgive myself for.

I looked up at the grotesque statue, still covered in the Starved's blood, where they'd sacrificed themselves and let it run for their dark ritual.

There was dried blood on the stone near my cheek, and I wondered if it was Kaitlyn's.

The rest of the space came into focus, different to how I'd last known it. The dank cavern had been dressed in plush carpets and throw blankets, velvet curtains and soft bedding, all red and gold like a romantic boudoir. Nearly two-dozen thralls stood idle around the walls, awaiting orders from their master and their mistress.

Adelle.

"Hello, Owen. I must say, I'd forgotten how pathetic you were as a human."

And there she was, standing with Dante beside the stone slab, looking down on me with cruel black eyes that stood out starkly against her icy-white skin and crystalline hair.

It was really her, back from the dead. "Fuck you, Adelle."

Adelle raised her eyebrows and looked to Dante.

"It's an insult," he clarified.

She looked amused, but her red smile dripped with hatred. "Indeed? How much you've caused me to miss out on."

She whistled, as though calling hounds, and some thralls approached. One had heavy chains in his hands, dragging them behind him.

"String him up," she commanded, pointing to the statue.

Dante turned his back on me as the thralls hoisted me off the slab and clamped the irons onto my wrists. He muttered, "We should kill him now, stop playing around. Then we can go after the woman. Her blood will destroy vampirekind, and we can't let that happen."

Adelle tapped a long nail against his chest. "You have no imagination at all, Dante, and you have no idea how disappointing that is."

Dante lifted his hands, as though at a loss. "We have the ring. Use it then, to kill him like he killed you, if you want to be creative about it."

My teeth clenched. I'd hoped the book and the ring it contained had been overlooked after the fight. Adelle and Dante having Tiamat's ring was all kinds of bad.

Like quiet worker ants, the thralls got the end of the chain up over the statue's neck then pulled, bringing me up by my wrists until my toes only just touched the ground.

Adelle kept her gaze locked on me, and smiled as the chain was secured.

"Oh no, he deserves worse than that. And I already

know just the thing." Adelle's fingers toyed down my chest, popping open all the buttons on my fight-torn shirt.

"Get your fingers off me, you filthy creature!"

Adelle gave me a practiced pout. She seemed amused by my insults, my useless thrashing, and just pressed her fingers closer to my bare skin. Her sharp nail cut the flesh of my sternum. The smell of my blood hit the air, and Adelle's tongue stroked across her full bottom lip.

Dante watched with a twitching jawline. "We don't have time for this. You act like you'd spare him out of love."

"Don't you *ever* mistake my actions as being those of love." Adelle whipped around to face him. Her feral expression softened instantly, becoming perfectly ladylike and demure. Her eyelids fluttered. "Dante, darling, you know I'm not interested in him like that. You are my one true love; you brought me back from the darkness, from dust."

She reached a hand behind his head and drew him into a long, deep kiss.

Then she turned her cheek to him, as though whispering in his ear, but speaking to me, "You will love what I have planned for Owen. It will destroy him over and over, and destroy that woman as well. First, I'm going to turn him. And then deny him the first feed vampires so desperately need. We will starve him to the point of insanity, and then we will set the woman he loves with the delicious blood in front of him."

Panic left me short of breath. My head shook.

Adelle's eyelids drooped, almost lustful. "And we will watch. We will watch him *tear her to shreds*."

A roar of sheer rage bellowed from my mouth.

My fingers curled and strained, and my body jerked, trying to snap my bonds. But they were solid iron. I was trapped. There was no way out.

"And when that woman's blood turns him human again, how you will *feel* her loss. I wonder just how much must be drunk from her to steal the gift of night from a vampire? Never mind, though, because when he changes, we will turn him again. After that, we will deliver him back to the Synedrion to be bound to the sun for his crimes. I'm sure when he's found with Tiamat's ring and Kaitlyn's blood all over him, they'll be more than happy to finish him off for us. As slowly as possible."

I prayed. I prayed for a miracle, for a savior, for the Ebonguard to burst into the room and deliver me from the terrible fate Adelle had planned. I prayed like I hadn't for centuries.

But it was too late.

Adelle's fangs punctured my neck, and all I could feel were pain and an icy sensation skidding underneath my flesh. I could feel my blood being drawn into her mouth, feel my veins collapsing. My heartbeat slowed and slowed again. She was taking me all the way to the brink of death.

I can't let this happen. I grasped onto that one wish, finding enough fight left in me to scream and thrash so wildly I broke free of Adelle's bite, tearing my neck wide open. Searing pain blinded me, and hard hands held me still—Dante, digging in his nails as Adelle returned her mouth to me, feeding in long, greedy gulps.

The sound of her contented sighs, washing through my ears and echoing down in my brain, were the last I knew as darkness took me.

Then it reversed.

I came back into a dim, gray awareness. Blood dripped into my mouth.

The darkness parted long enough for me to see Adelle's wrist, the long blue veins running along the shining white surface of her skin, the dark blood running into my mouth. I gagged and turned my head, but Dante's fingers gripped my temples and pushed me back.

I spat and flailed, trying to escape that rich, bloody flow coming from her arm. The thick drops splattered, landing hot and slick on my face. It coated my chin and cheeks, burning when it landed in my eyes.

I won't do this. I won't swallow it. I won't be turned.

I want to live.

But I could already feel the undead, cursed blood moving in my system, changing me, bringing me back from the very edge of death. I tried to hold onto my humanity, everything that made me human, the man Kaitlyn loved.

I tried to hold onto the feeling of my beating heart as the beating stopped.

I tried to hold onto the warmth of my skin as my flesh turned cold.

I tried to hold onto my love for Kaitlyn, that feeling, that unique and incredible *feeling*. But everything within me spiraled away. Even my shock and anguish felt as distant as the moon.

There was only pain, and death, and a hunger that built and burned in my veins, and a longing, lingering desire for …

Strawberry.

16

KAITLYN

I'd been summoned to the Synedrion council for an update on what had happened, then interrogated, as though I was the one who'd done something wrong.

The door to their chambers closed, hitting me on my ass on the way out. Literally.

The six remaining council members didn't care one bit that Owen was gone. They'd tested his blood. There was nothing in it that could be reverse engineered. Owen might have blabbed about the cure, but as long as I was still here, safe, with Heim on one side and some new Ebonguard on the other, never to be free again, they didn't care.

They didn't care when I pleaded for Joss's punishment to be revoked, that she didn't deserve it. They didn't care when I told them I was sure Adelle had

taken Owen, that she was sure to torture him. They didn't even care that Dante and Adelle had stolen Lance's "belonging." They were already criminals now, and that crime ranked way down on their list, under stealing relics of the original seven and using them to bring a vampire back from the dead.

Lance had stayed with me through the entire audience, after having found me weeping on the floor with Owen, Joss, and Dusky all gone. His eyes flashed with anger, and something more, when I told him about Joss hitting her three strikes and fleeing. Now, they wore the most haunted look I'd ever seen.

"This is my fault. I should have sent Dusky away. Before she turned on us."

"You'll have plenty of time to blame yourself later," I hissed. "How about you stow it and go get Owen back instead, since nobody else seems interested in doing it?"

"They are still looking for Adelle and Dante. If Owen is with them, like you believe, then he'll be recovered."

It didn't seem like they were doing enough. There had been no sign of hunting parties out searching, no alarms going off. It wasn't *enough*. I had to do something. I had to save him.

My words came from the very center of my aching heart. "You have to help me. You owe me for what you let happen, for letting Owen pay for your mistake.

You had to know that Dusky would do anything to be a vampire, to be with you, and you let her stay on because it was convenient for you to feed. You flirted with Joss in front of her—"

Lance raised his eyebrows.

"Don't pretend you didn't. You trampled all over Dusky's feelings. You used her, and never once thought about her."

The night of the ball, when Dusky was forgotten and left behind, was that when she met Adelle? I imagined it was, and I could also easily imagine what Adelle had promised Dusky in return for helping capture Owen. She would have promised Dusky the one thing Lance kept refusing her.

I laughed wryly. "I can't wait to see your face when Dusky comes back as a vampire, and comes after you."

Lance grabbed my arm and yanked me close to him, his mouth next to my ear. "Watch yourself, Kaitlyn. I can understand your hatred right now, but I'm not your enemy. Unless you want me to be."

His fingers were like hard steel bands on my flesh. His warning was the ringing of a bell.

"Release the human!" Heim barked.

Lance let go, holding up his hands in a peaceful gesture and taking a step back.

He was right. I hated them at that moment, even him. All of them. I hated them because the man I loved was gone and nobody cared. But I sure didn't need any more enemies.

"I'm sorry," I said.

"Me too. You know, I do care about Owen as well." Lance looked down. "He gave you the ring?"

I blinked at him, confused. *Tiamat's ring?* No. He meant the beautiful diamond ring I wore on the ring finger of my right hand. Lance mustn't have known about Tiamat's ring after all. "No. I found it. After … everything."

"Oh. He was so determined to go and get it for you."

My skin prickled all over. Owen should have been here. He should have been able to give the ring to me himself. I shook my head and slid down to the floor with my back against the door. "I thought he went for something else."

I lifted the diamond ringed finger close to my face and stared at it. I knew now he went to get this ring, that maybe he was going to … It was too painful to think about.

But maybe he got Tiamat's ring as well. Maybe he had it with him right now. Would it help him, if he did? I had no way of knowing. I didn't even know if he was still alive.

The diamond glinted, and I remembered the box it came in, and the small piece of paper inside it, both still in my pocket. I pulled the ring box out and unfolded the sheet, hoping for a handwritten note, a final love letter, a proposal, a magic spell to save and free us.

I frowned at the image in front of me. Just a printout of a badly taken photo of a sketch of a strange one-eyed face. A second eye had been drawn on in red pen over the top. What on earth did it mean?

"What is it?" Lance asked, crouching in front of me to look.

"I have no idea." My words were a harsh sob.

The door behind me suddenly opened, and I fell flat on my back. I just lay there, feeling useless and hopeless and exhausted, and stared up at Bertha's quizzical expression.

"What are you doing on the floor?"

I crumpled the paper in my hands, hoping she didn't see it, whatever it meant. I dabbed my eyes with it as though it were a tissue, then shoved it back in my pocket.

Bertha ignored my antics. "Listen, I've convinced the rest of the council that we should allow you to take a vision from Kissare's chalice. Dante and Adelle must be brought in, and it could help us. And it could help you if Owen is indeed with them."

"Really? Do you think it could show me where he is?" The chalice which showed visions of the future, like telling the Starved I was some kind of mythical baby-momma. I was intrigued, but skeptical. They'd said before, its visions were wildly open to interpretation. And the whole thing just stank of evil.

"Maybe. I think it's worth a chance. I think it's worth seeing what the chalice shows you."

Me with my stupid special blood. Me with all my *implications* for vampirekind. Of course she was interested in what the chalice would show me.

But if it could help me find Owen, I was in. I nodded sharply.

Lance extended a hand for me and helped me to my feet.

"Come on then," Bertha said, moving off at a brisk trot.

I felt out of place walking the halls of the Synedrion palace with Bertha in the lead, wearing what had to be a custom-sewn dress that made her look like a film star from the '40s, Lance in a suit, Ebonguard in their armor, and me in the jeans and hoodie I'd been in since leaving Owen that morning. Maybe vampires could always dress up because their general toughness meant they never got uncomfortable.

We went down stairs, and down more, through hallways lit with electric candles, where the décor wasn't as modern as it was in the plush and renovated main areas of the palace. We went deep into the oldest parts of the building, with the smell of damp limestone and aging tapestries hung from walls.

"Should I be knowing the way to where you keep this thing?" I asked. "You're not going to memory-wipe me after this?”

“The location of the reliquary is fairly common knowledge,” she said. “But only Synedrion members can get inside, so generally it’s safe.”

“Generally, until one of your own turns on you. How did someone like Dante get onto the council in the first place?”

“Sheer bloody luck,” Lance replied.

“Maybe not,” Bertha grumbled. “What with the mix of immortality and corruption, our government for many centuries has run on a sortition process. Any vampire who meets certain requirements can go into the draw when a seat becomes vacant. But I suspect the draw which appointed Dante was rigged. I have no idea how he did it, but I’m not the only one who suspects. That’s why we haven’t appointed a replacement for him yet, although we will have to soon.”

The hallway opened out into a formal entryway, with a very serious vault door guarded by equally serious Ebonguard. Bertha greeted them, and they cleared the way for her to approach a high-tech interface.

“This feels like the part in a spy movie before everything goes wrong,” I said, as Bertha had her fingerprint, retina, and voice scanned before a little light turned green and the door made chunky, sliding, mechanical sounds.

The inside of the vault was roomy, lined with

streaky white marble. The lights were dimmed, and the air was cool and dry. Four pedestals stood in a line. On one, Alam's dagger lay on a red velvet pillow. Two were empty. On the fourth was Kissare's chalice, looking just as it had the first time I saw it in the Scarl's monstrous hands.

All of the vampires with me paused, heads bowed, as though in a moment's silence. I twiddled my thumbs, awkwardly, waiting while trying to fight down the anxiety that was rising. I wasn't sure I even wanted to do this. Knowing the future always seemed alluring, but I was pretty sure it fell into the "be careful what you wish for" category. What if I saw the time and means of my own death? Not really something I wanted to know. But if there was a chance it could help me find Owen, I was in.

Bertha went to a side table where she picked up a silver jug. Lance looked at the empty pedestals.

"Thank the night Dante didn't take the chalice and dagger as well," he said.

Bertha returned, and poured some water into the ornate silver cup, inlaid with blood agate. "We think they only took the flute and veil because they didn't have time to put them back after using them. They've made themselves much greater criminals by taking our sacred relics."

I wondered again about Marduk's relic, what it was, and whether possessing it would be worth the risk of being hunted as a criminal for having it.

"Your hand, please." Bertha waited, her own hand outstretched for mine.

I reached out tentatively with my left. She gripped it hard, and swiftly punctured the tip of my finger with a sharp nail. I gasped, but she held tight, and squeezed a few drops of blood into the water in the goblet. *Drip, drip, drip.*

Red light shone out of the liquid, flickering and swirling.

My breath fluttered with fear.

Bertha took the chalice in her hands and held it before me. "Look into it," she instructed.

I gazed down. The few drops of blood had changed the water, thickening it to a dark red, viscous, rippling surface, lit from below. My belly rolled. I squeezed my eyes shut for a moment, breathed, found my courage, and looked again.

Think of Owen. Find Owen. I didn't know how this all worked, whether it could be directed, but I tried to focus my thoughts on him. I pictured his thick hair, and the little lines that had formed at the corners of his cornflower-blue eyes.

My heartbeat slowed, and my head swam. A strange languor filled me. The blood swirled against the sides of the cup, a whirlpool, parting to reveal the light below.

Images flashed straight into my mind, monochrome,

like a black-and-white film but all the black was red.

There was Owen. His face came into focus and so did mine. I could see us locked in an embrace, bodies moving together in passion, writhing. No … thrashing, panicked, fighting. No pleasure—only fear. Owen's teeth were in me, his fangs deep in my neck, my chest, blood dripped all around me, increasing the red of the already scarlet world.

All I could see was blood. My voice, filled with agony, unleashed screams of sheer pain and torment as Owen fed in feral, ravenous, shredding bites. A face watched over it all, large and strangely shaped, a carving with only one eye smiling in sick enjoyment. Then it winked another eye at me, light flashed, and a coin chinked and clattered, and twinkled as it hit the ground then disappeared under a pool of blood.

I scrambled backward. My legs went out from under me.

I was on the floor again, looking up at Bertha.

She knelt beside me. "What did you see?"

My head was shaking, trying to deny my words. "They're going to turn him. And he's going to kill me."

Lance's hand shook my shoulder so hard that my head lolled on my neck. "Where is he? Where, Kaitlyn?"

"All I saw was the two of us." And that face. The same face as the one on the paper Owen had left. It might be a clue to where he was, or to something more. That coin. I had to find it, but didn't want Bertha or the Ebonguard to know about it.

I struggled to my feet.

The vision still echoed in my head, snippets of trauma on replay. Lance put his arm around my waist and I sagged into him, drained and afraid that I couldn't escape the fate I'd just seen. It ate at me all the way back to his house, with no way of knowing if the cursed chalice had shown me a certain future, or just a vision of my deepest fears. But it had shown me that carved face, and it had shown me a coin. And that had to mean something. I kept that hope held tight and secret, because I knew no matter what, Owen and I didn't have much time left. Lin and Shirina had the Remortalis formula almost at testing stage. When it worked, they wouldn't need me anymore, and I knew, deep down, that they never intended to let me go.

Perhaps Owen killing me was just the solution all the vampires needed.

KAITLYN

Sunset tinged the mountains around us with a pink-orange glow, and I stared out the window at the eye-shaped Sun Shrine. The carved face, the winking eye, the note from Owen, all haunted me. It must mean something, and that shrine that Marduk himself built was involved. I knew it, and I knew I had to get there. I was going crazy with the need to act, but with Heim and another Ebonguard attached to each of my elbows, I could do nothing but go insane. They weren't even letting me go to the bathroom alone anymore.

I watched until the night turned blue and stars twinkled. My eyes ached in their sockets, but I couldn't sleep. In the kitchen across the living space, Lance brewed some coffee for me. He was trying extra hard to be helpful, and I wondered what else he could do, whether I could trust him with the knowledge of the face and the coin. If he would help me find it. But I couldn't even broach the subject with the Ebonguard here. So I stood and stared at the sky, as the fear of all being lost ate me from the inside. *Even if I can get away, how can I do this alone? How can I save Owen, myself, and our future?*

Everywhere I looked, all I saw was Owen's absence. His phone on the side table, and a shirt draped over a chair in our bedroom. The ring box and note in my pocket. The ring on my finger. My body kept swaying, like I expected to turn right into his arms.

But when I turned around, it was Joss who stood at the door. She had a black military pack over one shoulder, and her standard Ebonguard cowl was gone, replaced by a wicked expression.

"You came back," I gasped. I didn't know why she'd returned, but I was happy to see her.

Heim seemed weirdly happy too, in a much creepier way. "Didn't run away like a coward after all? Come back to receive your deserved punishment?"

"Fuck you, Heim," she said.

Heim and the other Ebonguard both bristled, but before they did anything, Joss sped over to Lance and threw him to the wall behind her.

Then she shot something straight at me.

I gasped, waiting for pain to strike, wondering why Joss had turned on me.

I did get her in this trouble, after all, a cold voice spoke in my head as a tiny canister exploded in the air.

Joss snatched a thick scarf up and over her nose and mouth, and the cloying, rotten scent of carrion filled the air, like she'd shot us with roadkill.

I choked on it, spat the disgusting fragrance from my mouth, but was otherwise unharmed. Heim and the other ebonguard hit the floor, deadweights as the corpse flower extract took its paralyzing effect.

My brain caught up with the situation, then my body a moment later, pushing the window behind me open to clear the gas from the air so any remaining scent didn't get to Lance and Joss across the room.

Joss nodded approvingly, then ran a kitchen towel under water and threw it to me. I moved across to the other side of the room and wiped myself as clean as I could from the spray of misted scent, but still kept my distance from Lance and Joss while my clothes aired out, as much as I could kiss Joss for relieving me of my bodyguards.

"Thank you. I've been trying to work out how to get rid of those guys. But why? How?"

"I wanted to help you." Joss slapped the pack on her back. "I never ran. I went to recover this. The vampire hunter's belongings."

"You said you couldn't find them," I said.

"I lied. I hid them so they wouldn't be confiscated. Thought I might need them." She hesitated. "I also went to find Dusky."

"Where is she? You didn't ..." I gulped, unsure what fate I wished on her.

"She's dead, but I didn't kill her. Adelle and Dante do have Owen, thanks to Dusky's help. They promised to turn her in return for it." She glanced over at Lance, and he dropped his gaze to the floor. "But they used her, drank from her, and dumped her on a hilltop, near death. That's how I found her. She told me everything before she died."

No, I didn't wish that fate on her. She was just young and dumb, and going after something she desperately wanted. I could relate to that. My nose scrunched up, and my eyes stung with angry tears. The poor girl. Even after what she did, she didn't deserve that. But I was starting to feel that Adelle and Dante deserved far worse.

I sat on the couch for a moment, pulling myself together. Lance joined Joss by the kitchen counter. "Glad to have you back," he said.

Joss's smile was too small to reach her eyes, but came quick and easy. Just how often had she smiled under her cowl, nobody but her aware?

My fingers clawed into the arm of the couch. "And Owen? Did you find out where they're holding him? If he's still alive?"

"I know where they were taking him. But I can't promise they will still be there when we get there."

"We?"

"We." Joss nodded. "If you want to go with me, that is."

"Damn straight I'm going."

"We're all in then," Lance agreed.

Joss touched his shoulder briefly. "You can still remain innocent, outside of this."

"And miss out on all the fun? I doubt it." He smiled roguishly.

Hope swelled inside me. This was my chance. *Our* chance. Owen wasn't dead. The chalice had shown him turned, feeding on me. If it was true, then at least he could be saved. And maybe I could change the future, with help.

Could I trust them? They were putting themselves in danger now, stepping outside the laws of their kind, for me and Owen and what they thought was right. Joss could have run and never come back, but she hadn't. *I think I can trust them.*

"There are some things we're going to need." I stood and walked toward them, but Joss held up her hands and I checked myself, staying where I was. I took the paper from my pocket, uncrumpled it, and held it out. "Owen left me this, and I think it has something to do with Marduk's relic. I also saw it in the chalice vision."

At Joss's questioning look, I filled her in on my trip to the vault with Bertha. "I saw this face, and a coin. Do you know where this sculpture is?"

Joss squinted at it. "It's in the Sun Shrine."

"I knew it."

Lance frowned at the crumpled printout. "You really think that's what it is, where it is? Marduk's relic?"

"I'm sure. And I'm sure we need it."

"A coin? It doesn't exactly sound dangerous, or useful. We have no idea what it does."

I raised my palms, exasperated. "A flute and a veil bring vampires back from the dead. If those chalice visions mean anything, we have to try."

"Agreed," said Joss. "I can go to look for it now, but we have to get moving. The Nemexia will keep those two knocked out for a while, but they are supposed to report in regularly, and as soon as they don't, we'll be in trouble."

Joss could probably zip in and out mostly unseen, thanks to her ninja-like abilities. She was fast and sly, and no doubt capable of a covert operation. But that was why I needed her to do something else.

"No. Lance and I will try to get the coin. I have another mission for you. If you choose to accept it."

I went over my plan with Joss.

If Owen was already turned, I had to be able to cure him. And I couldn't trust it to happen from drinking my blood again, not without him killing me. Lance had explained how ravenous vampires were right after being turned.

Deathless

The cure was still untested. It might not even work. But it might save me from Owen's hunger. Or, if all else failed, I could jab Adelle or Dante with it to even the playing field. Either way, we needed it. And only Joss could get it.

She looked thoughtful for a moment, hesitant, then nodded. "I can do that." She hoisted her pack of vampire-hunter toys back on and left.

Lance folded his arms, regarding me. "Ready to go treasure hunting?"

I put on my game face. "Always."

"You know this mightn't work. The cure, the relic—any of it. It's all a pretty slim chance at this stage."

"I know. I'm willing to risk it." A hand went to my stomach automatically. "I have to believe it will work. For all of us. Because what future do we have otherwise?"

Lance nodded slowly, staring wistfully toward the door Joss had just left by.

"What future indeed," he muttered.

I had to wonder too, what would happen to Joss after this? Whether she'd survive her mission I'd sent her on, and where she would go when this was over. If her kind would ever accept her back without punishment.

She'd chosen to help me. She had given me the chance I needed.

I only hoped it wasn't too late.

18

OWEN

I was empty, hollow. Claws of hunger scraped at the insides of the husk of my mind.

The pain of it twisted my limbs. My face contorted, my stomach clenched, my veins ached.

So hungry.

I tried to hold on to awareness. I tried to remember being human, feeling love. Tried to retain the lessons I'd learned as a human. *Be better. Humans aren't just food. Choose to do the right thing.*

But all I could feel was hunger, and thirst, and the overwhelming desire to sate myself. I couldn't reason anymore. Everything kept fading away into visions of blood, of feast, of the end to cravings. Of crimson flowing from a smooth column of neck, spilling thick across my fangs and parched tongue.

My body was strong again. I reveled in that strength. Why had I ever decided to stay human? Only some feeling made me think I wanted that, a feeling I'd forgotten. I could almost thank Adelle for changing me back, except I knew her reasons why.

"Damn it, Adelle. Free me!" I shook my arms in the chains that still held me, not strong enough to break free. "I must feed."

She floated into view and patted me like a child. "My, my, you seem hungry enough already."

I growled a response. I didn't even care anymore that she'd turned me. I kept telling myself I should, that I didn't want the result that she was hoping to achieve, but I'd lost the ability to care.

I'd heard and smelled Adelle feeding earlier. I'd screamed in rage and misery as the coppery scent of blood had filled the air, at the contented sounds Adelle made as she sucked at the human she had under her thrall. I was starving.

Adelle's laughter was low and taunting. "Don't worry. We'll feed you before you shrivel up like a Starved. We'll feed your love to you on a silver platter, unborn child and all. Can't you already taste her?"

My fangs were sharp against my bottom lip. I wanted Kaitlyn. But it was a dangerous sort of wanting. When I thought of her, and I thought of her constantly, all I could imagine was the deliciously sweet taste of her blood. Of how her blood, so rich and filled with life, reminded me of the ripe strawberries that grew wild under the bright sun.

That blood.

I wanted it.

I'd kill for it.

Adelle whispered cold breath into my ear, "We'll bring her to you soon, dear heart. Then you shall feed until you are full, and she is dead. I will see you destroy her, and yourself in the process. I long to see her blood turn you human again. How you will suffer then."

She walked away, over to a low table surrounded by plush cushions and blood-drained thralls. She picked up a flute, Ri's flute, and twirled the ancient carved wood in her fingers. "But you must be a vampire to be bound to the sun. Isn't it lucky we have so many options now? I can punish you as human and as vampire, drive you insane with emotions, then burn you in the sun, over and over. Then I can even return you from true death. We could do this forever, my love."

"I killed you once, Adelle. I can kill you again."

Her shrill laughter echoed through the stony cavern.

Dante walked out from somewhere behind me and the huge statue I was chained to. He snarled. "Are you sure this is only for revenge, *my love*? He will have to die; you know that. You should want that."

Jealous fool. "She always did like me best." I managed a hunger-weak grin.

Dante took my throat in his hand, as though he would rip my head off. I clung to one final straw of reason that told me that would be for the best. Then I wouldn't be driven to kill Strawberry.

No. Her name is Kaitlyn, she's an actress, she loves food, she loves me, and I love her. I recited the lines to myself to try to remember, but they were only words.

"Let him go, fool. You have nothing to fear from him. He's only still alive for our entertainment. Only until we can bring that woman here for him to feed upon."

"If she can even be found."

Adelle chuckled. "She will be. She will come to him, one way or another."

Dante sniffed, as though he hardly cared, and released my throat. My dry, aching throat.

So hungry …

Memories of my first turning toppled through my thoughts, reminding me of hunts and blood, and times and people long dead. I groaned and thrashed. A fever, an animal bloodlust rode through me, making my head spin and my hands clench into fists. My nails tore at my palms, but released no pain, no blood. Adelle bled me nearly dry and gave me just enough blood to turn me but not enough to sustain me.

I'd be mindless soon.

I had to remember. I had to remember that her name was Kaitlyn and that I loved her. That she was carrying our child and our future within her.

My body shriveled against my shrinking heart.

Her name is …

Strawberry. She was a ripe and delicious strawberry, begging to be consumed. And I could think of no reason why I shouldn't. I couldn't think at all.

19

KAITLYN

Long dewy grass wet my ankles as Lance and I dashed to his car. It would have been faster and more inconspicuous for him to carry me, since the shrine was just up the hill from his estate, but he worried my hair or clothes were still wafting with Nemexia. I couldn't smell it anymore myself, but it wasn't a risk we could take right now.

Lance took the driver's seat and I jumped in the back, carrying a clean sweater and jeans I'd snatched on the way out. Lance grabbed the wheel, turned off all automated safety restrictions on the touchscreen, then sped along the curving mountain road.

I did my best not to crash about as I got changed while taking hairpin bends at a breakneck speed. Lance opened the front windows to keep fresh air

streaming through.

"What do I need to know about this place? Is it guarded? Boobytrapped? Full of snakes?" I asked, wriggling my hips into the tight denim.

Lance kept his eyes on the road, and the amphitheater that surrounded the Sun Shrine came into view. "Might be guarded. There are monks dedicated to the shrine's rituals and protection who may be around. We'll have to work out a way to get past them."

"On it," I said. I tugged the sweater over my head and realized I'd grabbed one of Owen's instead of mine. It swam against my skin, and I hugged it there.

"I'm not really sure what to expect. I've avoided attending the ceremonies, including the most recent one for the Starved," Lance said. "It's not the sort of place vampires are dying to break into though."

I wondered how many break-ins the lethal injection rooms of human prisons had to deal with. But they weren't hiding ancient powerful artifacts.

Lance reached for something in a bag he'd brought with him, then handed it back to me. A wooden stake, made of wickedly sharp, pointed hardwood. "Here. I'm not going to use it. I don't want to risk spending the rest of my life in the Sun Shrine for killing other vampires. But you should have it." Then he muttered, "Not that what we're doing tonight isn't treasonous enough."

"Thanks," I said, and meant it. He was risking a

lot to help me, and in return I'd try to keep as many crimes directly off him as I could.

I shoved the stake into my back pocket. I felt like a character in some movie I hadn't acted in yet, and I embraced the role. Courageous Kaitlyn. Adventurous Kaitlyn. Bulletproof Kaitlyn. I was a good actor. I could be those things tonight. I could save Owen. Why did I ever think me and my acting were weak? I could do anything, be anything I needed to be. And tonight, I'd be the kick-ass treasure hunter who would find the magical artefact and tear any enemy that stood in my way to the ground.

We drove in through open gates to a small parking lot.

Outside, we could see down into the amphitheater, and make out a single golden-robed figure standing near the entrance to the ancient central temple.

"Wait for my signal. I have a plan," I said, hopping out of the car.

I wandered down the weather-smoothed stone steps toward the shrine's guardian. He watched me all the way, but didn't move. He kept his back to the massive stone slabs and dark opening behind him.

I hugged the bundle in my arms.

"Night's greetings," I said cheerfully. As I grew close, I saw that the bottom hem of his gown was a dull gray.

"And to you." He looked me up and down, and

inhaled through his nose. "Apologies, but the Sun Shrine is not open to visitors at this time."

I looked as disappointed as I could until I was right in front of him, within reach, then I shoved my bundle of dirty clothes in his face. He seemed simply insulted at first, and I hoped there was enough Nemexia left on them to knock the guy out.

He struggled, pushing the clothes away. Lance sped down to us and took hold of the monk's arms from behind, and we both fought for a long moment to keep the scent-laced clothing against his mouth. Finally, I felt the golden-clad monk weakening. He drooped, slowly, slowly, like a woozy drunk, until we could lay him onto the stone at our feet. We left the clothes there with him, close to his face so he wouldn't wake up again and surprise us during our search.

"Let's hope he was the only one," I said, and we stepped in through the largest gap between the megaliths that formed the outer curved walls of the shrine.

Up close, they were more like a series of linked dolmens than a solid wall, giving lots of spaces for sunlight to flow in that lined up again to more small vertical holes cut into the solid inner wall of the circular center. The limestone was pockmarked from the weather, the moonlight making it look silver and cratered like the moon itself.

We had to duck low to go through the entrance

into the main chamber. Inside was dim and musty, with not enough light to see by. Lance pulled a flashlight from his bag and handed it to me. I clicked it on and shone it around the space.

Before us was a mountain of ashes.

I gagged. "I thought you said those monks maintained this place. When was the last time they cleaned?"

"I said protected, and that includes the ashes. When a vampire is bound to the sun, their ashes are never cleaned away."

The ash filled the room, curving in swathes up the walls. Paths had been tracked in it here and there, leading to manacles which were barely visible on the walls under more ash. I took a tentative step forward, and my shoe sunk into the ash like it was the softest of snow. I pulled the neck of Owen's sweater up over my nose and mouth, trying to block the burnt smell.

I turned a circle in the space. Just this single, round room. The wall was made up of massive stones, and the roof had a secondary raised dome in the center, but there wasn't much else to see. "Where is the face? Marduk's face?"

Lance tipped his head toward the largest of the megaliths directly across the room from the entrance, through the deepest stretches of ash. "Should be right over there."

"Ugh, I think I would have preferred snakes." I stepped forward, and by midway across the room

I was wading through ash up to my thighs. My clothing turned gray and stiff, and my skin dried at the touch of it.

Lance stalked along behind me, silently, placing his footsteps in the holes I had made.

Something clamped onto my ankle. I clenched my teeth, swallowing my scream. I stumbled backward into Lance, and he grabbed onto me, pulling me back. My foot was still trapped, dragging the ashes and whatever was beneath along with it. Through the shifting dust, a skeletal hand wrapped around me. I kicked at it with my other foot.

More ash cleared, revealing the hand of one of the Starved. It was so emaciated it must have fallen free of its shackles and become lost, too weak to move, in the sea of vampire remains.

Its body twitched beneath a tattered robe. Its sewn-together lips ground against each other, dry as dirt. I wondered just which one it was, whether it was one of the ones who had captured me, or pinned me down on the sacrificial altar, or danced and chanted awaiting the terrible things they wished for me and my body.

I managed to shake my ankle free of its grasp, and it just lay there on the floor. It was as close to death as an immortal creature could be, and suffering more than anything deserved to suffer.

Lance's voice was hushed. "Just ignore him. He's

no threat."

It was true. He didn't even have the strength to drag himself across the floor to attempt anything.

I said in a sibilant whisper, "No, I'll deal with this."

Lance didn't question me as I drew the stake from my back pocket, didn't ask if I was sure. He knew I was.

I stood over the Starved, the stake held firm in both hands.

The Starved lifted a quivering finger, and his dirty nail split the stitches that held his lips shut. A single word wheezed from his mouth, *"Please."*

"Yes," I said as gently as possible. I lifted the stake high, then drove it downward in one long, smooth stroke that split his chest open and found what remained of his decayed heart. He curled up around the stake, like some alien caterpillar, then ash flaked off, drifting away to join the rest around us. The robe collapsed onto a pile of shrunken, bleached bones that disintegrated into nothing with a soft whooshing sound.

I stared for a moment longer, then blinking the ash from my eyes, I retrieved the stake.

Lance cleared his throat and put a hand over his chest. "I'm not entirely sure anymore if giving you the stake was a good idea."

"Maybe Joss and I can both join the vampire hunters after all this is done."

Lance looked even more conflicted.

"You don't want her to go, do you?" I asked.

"No. But I can't ask her to stay, either. Not with the punishment awaiting her."

"What's it like, to care about someone when you're a vampire?" I was genuinely curious.

"We don't. Not really. Not the way humans do. We *want* things. But we don't often care what damage our wants cause, as long as we get what we want." Lance grinned roguishly. "Which is why it's understandable that Owen gets jealous of me. If I wanted you, not much would get in my way."

"Yeah, I'd be getting in your way, for starters," I countered, pointing my stake at him.

"I don't want you though. Not like that. What I've wanted is the love you show. I've been jealous of you and Owen, seeing you together, what your love has been capable of. I want that. And I find myself wanting Joss. But I'm not sure where that leaves me, since I also want to remain a vampire."

"Conflicting wants? That actually sounds pretty human to me." I turned the stake around, holding the blunt end outwards. I placed my hand on Lance's shoulder. "What I want right now is to find this damned coin. Thank you for being here, and helping me."

"As long as I live unpunished to tell the tale, you're welcome. Otherwise, we'll have words."

Taking the stake as a bat to the ash in front of me,

Deathless

I moved through with long strides, clearing the way until I reached the wall. The ash was thicker against the stone, almost as though the cinders had fused against it, but I used the stake and my hands to scrub it clear, and soon found the rough shape of Marduk's head, carved underneath. The face was as tall as I was, and even though worn and misshapen with dusty residue, its expression was twisted in evil pleasure.

Lance shook his head at it. "Still watching the victims of the torture he designed after all these years."

It looked at me with two eyes, but the sketch of it Owen gave me only had one. I checked the copy again, and Owen had drawn a second eye on the right side in red pen. I dug and scratched all around that eye, but couldn't see anything other than stone.

I grunted in frustration.

"Let me have a go," Lance said. He stepped forward, made a fist, and jabbed swiftly at that right eye. "I never liked that guy."

The stone cracked, crumbling away.

A small chamber sat behind it, and within, the glint of gold.

"All yours," he said. "Not a chance I'm touching that thing."

All my bravado faded away at the sight of the coin within that small stone hollow. All my courage crumbled in the face of this ancient item that could make or break my future.

For all I knew, I was the one who would burn to a crisp upon touching it. I had to hope it did something that only affected vampires, not humans. I had to trust I was shown this coin in the chalice vision for a reason.

I don't have to act the part. I am brave.

I took a deep, steadying breath, and reached my hand in, wrapping my fingers around the cool gold.

I closed my eyes, counted to ten, and found myself still whole.

The coin was small in my palm, unevenly round, stamped with a stylized eye.

I blew out a whistling breath. "Okay, we found it. Now what?"

20

KAITLYN

We left Lance's car up a quiet back road, under the cover of an ancient pine tree. After a sniff of my hair to confirm he wasn't going to pass out, he scooped me up and ran us to the meeting point we'd arranged with Joss.

The small cabin sat on a rocky slope. The moon illuminated untended fields edged with toppled stone walls. Lance told me this was where he'd taken Owen when he'd rescued him from where the Starved kept us before. An old, abandoned farmhouse, within walking distance of where Adelle had Owen—the very same place.

No way did I ever want to go back there, into that dark cave system where we were nearly destroyed by the Starved. But I would. I was going to march right in there to save Owen. As soon as I could make this damn coin do something.

I sat in the musty cabin alone, trying all sorts of things to get the coin to work. Lance waited outside, unwilling to be around for whatever was about to happen. The danger level didn't seem high though. It felt like hours had passed, and I had nothing.

I tried pointing the coin like a gun, throwing it at things, holding it against my head and thinking really hard. I reopened the scab from the chalice vision and bled on it. I searched the coin under torchlight for symbols or clues. I held it against my eyes. I whispered wishes and magic words, abracadabra alakazam, worketh-you-fuckingeth-thingeth.

The rickety chair I sat on wobbled as I stomped my feet. "Come on!"

I needed more ideas. *Why didn't this thing come with instructions?*

Maybe it only worked in combination with something else, like the flute and veil. Maybe it only worked when actually targeted at a vampire, but I wasn't going to test it on Lance.

Maybe it didn't work at all.

I thumped my forehead on the wooden table. Dust puffed up around me.

Voices came from outside. Lance was talking to someone, and then the door opened just a little. I pointed my torch and squinted.

"Joss? You made it!"

"All clear?"

"Yeah, just me and a useless chunk of gold. I swear I'm going to pawn this thing when I get back to the human world."

The door creaked as Joss came through. She was wearing her full Ebonguard uniform including the cowl, looking covert and kickass.

"Lance, you can come in too if you want. This coin isn't doing anything."

"I'm good out here, thanks," he called back.

Joss held up a clear sample bag with a couple of syringes in it. "Got it."

The Remortalis. "At least your mission was a success."

"Partially. These samples were ready for testing, but haven't yet been trialed."

"So we've got a useless coin, and some scientific concoction with unknown results? We are so winning right now."

Joss came closer and peered down at the coin on the table. "Marduk's coin. You really found it. Amazing." She reached for it, then seemed to think better and stepped back.

"It would be amazing if it did something," I grumbled. "Sorry for being a grump. Thank you for getting the cure."

She shrugged, as though it was no big deal. But

I knew it was. She'd put her whole existence on the line for me.

"And I'm glad you made it back safe. That you came back to help us at all—it means so much, and I know you've sacrificed a lot because of me."

Only Joss's eyes were visible, making it hard to judge her expression. She walked around to the other side of the table but didn't sit down. "I think I realized early on that I was becoming more loyal to you than I was to my orders. That was why I hid the hunter's gear. I knew I needed options, being so close to three strikes and knowing an order might have come that I couldn't or wouldn't follow."

"Like when you said you'd kill me if ordered to?" I smirked.

Joss chuckled. "Like that. I feel like you've changed me. Maybe just being close to you for extended periods, just the scent of your blood, is enough to produce sensations of empathy."

Lance called in through the open door, "There might be something to that. It's been so long since I fed from you, but I still feel … different."

"And I have never fed from you," Joss pointed out, as though it were a contest.

"Did you vampires ever think it could be nothing to do with blood?" I sighed. "There are human studies that show simply being treated kindly, or witnessing empathy, makes people more empathetic. Could it be that I'm not magically changing you, but just changing your minds? I mean, I know scientifically my blood does something. But ideas are powerful too."

"That they are," Joss agreed.

And here I had been feeling useless and weak for being human. But it was the parts of me that were human, my ideals and morals, and ability to feel love and empathy, that had brought Joss and Lance to my side as allies. Maybe even friends.

I lifted the coin from the table and balanced it in the palm of my hand. "Although, ideas aren't exactly going to help much when the Synedrion catches up to us, having escaped and stolen their precious relic. And they aren't going to help get Owen back from Adelle and Dante."

Joss leaned against the edge of the table. "We might have to give up on that coin, make a plan around using the Remortalis. I can try to get Owen out of there, and if he's turned, bring him back here for the cure."

"It would be three vamps plus who-knows-what-else against one," I said. "I can't let you go and do that alone."

"Neither can I," Lance agreed from outside.

"And if Owen's turned, will he be willing to go with you?" *Will he be at all the man I remember? Will he be the cold, calculating creature who imprisoned me? Or will he be something else?*

Concern flashed over Joss's eyes. "Hard to say."

"And the Remortalis might not work. It might take too long, and Adelle and Dante or the Synedrion could find us at any moment. This is only going to work if we can take out Adelle and Dante, and I can't ask you guys to stack that onto your list of crimes for helping me."

"We could go to the Synedrion for help," Lance called in.

I snorted. "Us criminals? They haven't helped us at the best of times, and if Owen has been turned, I might lose my only chance to turn him back." I eyed the pack that had belonged to the Blade of Alam. "Got any Nemexia left?"

"Nope, used the last of it getting out of the lab."

And the sunlight gun had disappeared into the forest after the fall and was probably smashed to bits. "Absinthe Molotov cocktails? Anything?"

Joss shook her head.

"Then we sneak in, you guys jab Adelle and Dante with the Remortalis, and I let Owen feed on me until he changes back to human. Then we get our asses out of there."

"No," Joss said firmly. "I could only get two doses. And I'm keeping one of them."

"What?"

Joss straightened up and walked over to the other

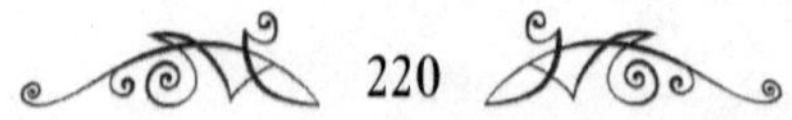

side of the room, her back turned. "I don't know what's going to happen after this. I want to help you get Owen back, but after that, I have to go my own way. I cared for you too much, and I've lost my whole identity for it. Being an Ebonguard was my life. And I can't be that anymore. I might not even be able to be a vampire anymore. So I'm keeping one of the doses. I don't know if it works, or if I'll have to use it, but at least I can use it as leverage, a bargaining chip, if I need to."

I didn't want to admit she was right, that it was only fair, that I knew she couldn't easily get her hands on more, that the Remortalis was as valuable to her future as it was to mine. I had to do something. I didn't know for certain if Owen had been turned or not, but either way they'd be torturing him. Every moment we wasted here, he suffered.

I was so frustrated I said, "I tell you what. We'll flip for it. Heads, you win and keep one of the doses. Tails and let me have it, and we do my plan and work out the rest later."

Joss turned around and glared at me. "This isn't up for—"

Before she could finish her sentence, I flipped the coin into the air.

The coin flew up, flipping over and over in the dim light, hovering and spinning.

Gaining speed. Not falling back into my waiting hand.

A brilliant blast of light erupted from the coin. Everything stood out in sharp, stark relief, bright light and black shadows, before even that was lost and there was only burning white.

Joss was screaming. Outside, Lance was screaming.

My skin grew hot, and my eyes watered, eyelids screwed shut but still stinging from the blast. I tried to duck but there was no escape. It was like a nuclear weapon had gone off, or a new sun had been born within that room.

The coin landed on the floor with a bell-like tinkle, but I still couldn't see. The light dimmed, slowly, and my vision swam with burned-in spots. I smelled smoke.

"Joss!" I screamed.

21

KAITLYN

"Joss!" I cried out again when there was no answer. "Lance?" I yelled, needing his help, and hoping he was there to give it. No reply.

I blinked, trying to get my vision to clear. There was no need for the torch, as a low level of light still lingered and reflected around the room, as though re-absorbing into the coin.

When I spotted the smoking mound of Ebonguard uniform, my first instinct was to turn back the other way and run as fast as I could. The stench of burning was unbearable.

But then she shifted, moaning. The sound of her agony split my eardrums. *What have I done?*

I ran to Joss and landed on my knees beside her. Then I heard Lance shouting from outside, cursing.

"Don't come in, there's still light, and Joss is …"

He appeared at the door, slouching and singed, smoke drifting from his clothes. He held his arm up over his face, and even the low light in the room made his skin bubble and blister. Then he was kneeling beside us, scooping his arms under Joss.

"Get back outside," I cried.

He stumbled, his face riddled with agony. He lagged, burning more with each step. Even my human skin felt hot all over, red and raw, like I had a bad sunburn. I put my shoulder against Lance and helped push the two of them outside into the cool night air.

The three of us landed in the grass. I coughed and choked, the terrible, charred, fatty smell of burned flesh filling my lungs.

It was a nightmare. Joss had stopped screaming. She just twitched beneath the armor that should have protected her. That *had* protected her from normal daylight. It was the only reason she was still here at all.

Lance wheezed out, "What just happened?"

"I finally figured out how the coin works. And I wish I hadn't."

Lance's face was red-raw, peeling like a bad sunburn, but flaking ash instead of flesh.

"Are you going to …" I didn't know a polite way to ask if someone was about to spontaneously combust.

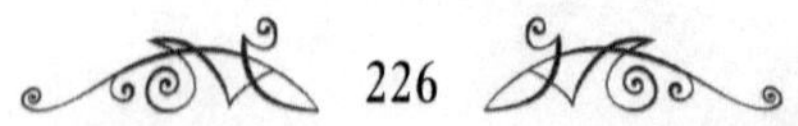

"I'll heal. It's just the surface. Not sure about Joss though."

He leaned over close to her, pulling away her cowl in a flurry of gray flakes. He covered his mouth, as though he might vomit. "Her eyes. They're gone."

"Gone?" I squeaked. I couldn't even bring myself to look.

"Burnt right out. Fuck. She needs blood, and now, if she has any chance of regenerating."

My mouth hung open as all the implications of Lance's words flew through my mind. Because I was the only human there. "You know what my blood might do to her."

"She's past the point of regenerating on her own. She needs blood now, or she'll keep turning to ash. She just needs a little, to regenerate enough to stop the burning."

If I did this, then maybe I could fix it. "A small amount shouldn't be enough change her," I reasoned, talking myself into it. "Okay. Okay. I'll do it." My voice shook and broke. The idea I was going to willingly offer myself up to her fangs knocked my heart into high gear.

"I'll stop her when she's had enough."

"You better," I warned. It wasn't just me at risk; it was the baby too. I doubted Lance would be able to pull Joss off me if she were at her full strength. But right now, she barely seemed alive.

Lance took my wrist and placed it against Joss's mouth, or what remained of it. I still couldn't look. But I could feel crumbling ash over sharp fangs.

Nothing happened. Lance forced my wrist against Joss's teeth, puncturing them with his pressure, and I stifled a cry.

Then my blood flowed. Slowly at first, and then a strong suction built through my veins. The pain was intense, and dizziness swirled through me.

The remains of her lips around my wrist began to change, shifting and regrowing, and she let out a feral growl.

Her hands came up, still in black gloves, and joined Lance's grip on my arm. I panicked, trying to struggle away. "Enough. Stop!"

Lance let go of me and pried Joss's hands away, then pulled my wrist from her mouth.

She reeled, trying to claw her way back to me, wanting more. I finally looked at her face, a sickeningly twisted mix of ash and regrowing flesh and flecks of blood. I still couldn't see her eyes under it all.

Lance dragged her up off the grass, taking her back into the cabin where the light had completely subsided. He fought to pull her through the main room into the bedroom, the only other room in the small building. He shut the door behind them. Thrashing and crashing and fighting sounds burst through the walls.

Deathless

I sat on the damp ground, put pressure on my ravaged wrist, and tried not to weep.

Time passed, and the sounds from the room stopped. The night felt like it had gone on forever, and I wanted to lay down in the dewy grass and sleep, but I couldn't. Not now I had the coin, and the cure, and at least one of them worked.

I staggered inside, then fell back to my knees again in the cabin, crawling around to recover the coin. It had landed just under the seat I'd been sitting on before, and I picked it up delicately then squeezed it into my palm, pressing it there, as though making it a permanent part of myself.

I went to the bag Lance had brought and rummaged through it, almost weeping again to see he'd thrown some food in there for me. Just a handful of individually wrapped cake treats, but they were like sugary cloudy bliss to eat, and replenished some energy. I scoffed them all down in an instant.

I was still unsteady on my feet, but I couldn't wait any longer. It was time to go after Owen.

I lifted my hand to knock at the door when I heard a voice coming through.

"I'm sorry. I could have let you drink more, but I didn't want …"

I held my breath, waiting, and hoping for a reply.

"I understand. You didn't want me to change, but I am changed."

Joss. She was alive, conscious, talking. But changed? Surely, she didn't drink enough to turn her human.

"It might not be permanent," Lance offered.

The first drink shouldn't be. It hadn't been with Lance. But what if my blood had gotten stronger? No one had drunk from me since I became pregnant.

"What color are they?" Joss asked. "My eyes?"

I couldn't bear it, and pushed through into the room to see for myself.

Joss sat on the edge of the bed and turned to the sound of me coming in, but didn't look directly at me. Her normally black vampire eyes were the gray of an overcast summer.

"Kaitlyn?" she asked, as though confused.

"Yeah, yeah, it's me."

She blinked. Her eyes shifted again to find my voice, and it hit me.

She's not human. She's blind. Her eyes, her skin, had all regrown, but not fully recovered. Her hair was still pink around the back, but the front was all a dark brown, grown back in its natural color.

"I'm so sorry," I said.

Her expression held a vulnerability I'd never seen before. But I was still getting used to seeing her face.

"I'm fine. Really. Ebonguard are trained to be just as efficient without our eyesight." She flinched a little on the word Ebonguard. We all knew she

wasn't that anymore.

"You might still regenerate fully, in time," Lance said softly. He was mostly healed too, but there were still some raw spots on his hands and face that I had to look away from.

The question of what would happen if her eyesight didn't regenerate dropped us all awkwardly into silence.

Joss's lips grew tight. "Stop looking at me like that."

"Like what?"

"I don't know, but I can tell you're looking. I will be fine. You two go, go and use that damned coin on someone who deserves it."

"I'm staying," Lance said.

"I don't need your help," she argued.

"I'm sure you don't. But maybe you need some company. Just until your eyesight comes back." Lance glanced over at me, and I nodded. Someone should stay with her. This wasn't the time to be alone, even for someone like Joss. He smiled at me. "Also, I have no intention of ever being around you and that coin, if you are going to use it again."

"Same," said Joss.

"Fair enough," I agreed. "You two have helped so much already. I've got this now."

I hesitated for a moment, then stepped forward and hugged Lance, and then Joss, squeezing her extra tight. Lance walked me to the door and pointed the way, and in the far distance I could just make out

the little mud-brick cottage that I recognized, and that held the entrance to a world of terror beneath.

The temperature had dropped, a strong northerly wind blowing frost through the air, and I shivered. Lance gave me his jacket. "Good luck."

"Thanks. See you soon … I hope."

I picked up one of the Remortalis syringes, and the coin, and put the stake in my back pocket, then took to the road. I slushed through the long grass and along worn goat tracks. There was a brush of color on one rim of the horizon, a rosy-pink glow of hope, and promise of future days.

And now, I carried my own sun in the palm of my hand. I only hoped I wouldn't have to use it on Owen to protect myself and our baby. Some of the scenes the chalice showed me have proven to be true. I helped make them become reality, but could I keep shaping the future? There might be no escape from the other horrors shown in that blood-red vision.

22

KAITLYN

As I walked, I plucked some stitches free in an inside hem of Lance's jacket and placed the syringe and coin into the inner lining. I was about to hand myself over to a den of evil, and I didn't want my only chances of survival taken from me. I just had to get in as far as I could, use the cure on Owen, then flip the coin. *Sure. Easy.*

The coat was too big for me, and it hung loosely from my narrow shoulders. I drew it closer as I reached the tumbledown cottage. Dead vines clustered around the walls, and the smell of something old and dirty rose from the tunnel inside. The wind smelled sour and bitter, like even nature knew there was something awful here, something evil.

The lair of the Starved.

A thrall stood at the entrance, guarding with glazed eyes. His sun-worn skin and strong hands were those of someone who had farmed his whole life. When I moved near him, he grabbed my wrist and started shambling down into the tunnel.

"You can let go. I'm going that way anyway," I said. But I knew he could hear no one but his masters, nothing but their orders. I was an intruder, and I would be taken to them.

At least I wouldn't have to wander the torch-lit tunnels aimlessly on my own.

We went past the dungeon, the cells Owen and I had once been kept in, and the tunnel led from there in a direction I knew. The way to the main chamber, with the hideous, massive statue, and the stone altar. I tried to prepare myself for what I would find there, for even being in that space again.

And then we were there.

"Isn't this cozy," I muttered.

Adelle and Dante lounged together on a low make-shift bed, amongst piles of plush cushions in reds and golds. My approach ended their game, which had been flicking drops of what looked like blood out of a bowl toward the howling, feral, nightmare version of the man I loved. Their attention shot my way as the thrall dragged me toward them.

Fangs bared, Owen turned his attention to me as well. He inhaled a long, deep breath, then went wild, jarring at the chains that held him in place, dangling from the same statue I'd once been bound to.

That was it. He was turned. He was a vampire. A taunted, tortured, and starved vampire. His cheeks were sunken in, his eyes were dark, and I could see the hunger all over him. And here I was, walking in as the most delicious thing he had known in four hundred years.

Owen … I hope this works.

"What do we have here?" Adelle looked honestly surprised.

"Didn't mean to interrupt. Actually, no, I did. That's why I came." I shook my wrist free of the thrall, who seemed happy to let me go now I'd been noticed by his masters. His job complete, he wandered away.

Dante got to his feet and growled. "How did you find us?"

"She's a sly one." Adelle slowly raised herself, looking me over. "But it saves us having to go and bring you in. Isn't that nice? We were going to wait until Owen was even hungrier, but I think he's probably hungry enough."

I nodded, already knowing what she alluded to. "You turned him, starved him, and were going to make him feed on me. Get your petty revenge. And then what? Be on the run for the rest of your immortal lives? Until Adelle turns on you too, Dante, of course."

Adelle snapped her fingers and the thrall came back. "She's awfully cocky. Search her for weapons."

The thrall patted me down awkwardly, and found the stake that was jutting from the back pocket of my pants. He yanked it out and tossed it away into the corner of the room. Good. I'd left it there as a decoy. I didn't need it anyway.

Adelle seemed amused by my pointy stick. She wandered over to a table and leaned on it, picking up a very old-looking black veil and toying with it. "Come on then. Let's begin the show, shall we?"

She made a little shooing noise with her mouth, and gestured with her eyes.

I did as she wanted. I forced myself to walk forward, bringing myself closer and closer to the being of only fangs and bloodlust in front of me. Owen. But not Owen. A monster in the body of the man I loved. My body shook violently as I looked upon everything I had been afraid of.

Dante walked over to Adelle and wrapped an arm around her waist, lust in his eyes. "Smell that warm, ripe human flesh, Owen. So easily torn, so easily parted with your teeth to reveal the sweet nectar inside. Doesn't it just drive you insane?"

Adelle loosed a high-pitched giggle as Dante mimicked feeding on her neck.

I ignored them, edging carefully toward my goal.

"Owen?" My voice cracked, shattered. I tried to

hold it together. "You in there at all?"

His only reply was gnawing, frothing, bestial rage.

"Do you remember me? Or this?" I held up the ring I wore, that he'd left for me. "Or this?" I placed that hand over my belly.

Nothing in his expression changed. His shirt was gone, and every muscle was tensed to the extreme. The chains groaned as he strained toward me. With a metallic screech, one chain broke free. He swiped his newly freed hand at me, clawing the air an inch in front of my nose.

Adelle cheered and Dante applauded.

I flinched, but held my ground. There was no reaching him now. The coin was my secret weapon, but I couldn't use it yet or he would burn. I wouldn't do that to him. The man I loved was still there, somewhere, under the vampire curse and the hunger.

I reached into the inner lining of the jacket, took the syringe in one hand, and the coin in the other.

"Owen? I love you." I stabbed the syringe into his chest and pushed the plunger. He roared, and broke his final chain.

He stood there, staring down at the thing sticking out of his torso.

Adelle yelled, furious, "What is that? What are you doing?"

Owen brushed the syringe away, shook his head, locked eyes with me, and growled.

Then he lunged at me.

Nothing. I did nothing. It didn't work.

I staggered backward, trying to get away, but Owen pounced upon me like a jungle cat, and I hit the mountain of cushions behind me. Adelle's laughter echoed throughout the huge chamber. Owen took his first tearing bite of my neck, plunging his teeth in deeper than I'd ever known.

I screamed.

"No, Owen, no!" I tried to push him off. Tried to fight. He pinned me to the floor, gulping so fast my whole body convulsed.

Adelle came closer. The image of her seemed to swim, wavy between the dark patches that overtook my vision. "Yes, oh yes, this is beautiful." She twirled the veil in her hands, placed it on her head, and skipped around, as the man I loved tried to drink every last drop of my life.

Tears flowed faster than my blood and I knew what I had to do. I had to live. And that meant every vampire in this room had to die.

Including Owen.

My arm was outstretched on the floor, stuck under Owen's body. The coin within my palm was hard and warm from my skin. I just hoped I had the strength to flick my wrist ...

I wailed in pain, in grief, as the coin flew from my fingers, up into the air above Owen as he fed. Lying on my back under him, as the world faded away, I saw it hover, spinning, faster and faster. And then all the world was light.

And pain.

And fire.

Above me, Owen burned. He reeled back and off me, curling into a ball, turning gray, flaking away.

Bright and harsh like the outlines of distant suns, Adelle and Dante went up in flames, crumbling into ash.

The light filled every space, but darkness had entered me, filled me whole, and I faded. Light and dark competed to steal my existence. The last thing I saw was the coin landing in a pool of my own blood.

23

OWEN

Everything hurt. I folded in on myself. Flesh on fire. Hunger burning away, from all-consuming to consumed by agony. I could only think one thought …

This is … finally … the end of me.

And then the smallest flutter. A lurching pressure in my chest.

Bu-bump.

Bu-bump.

I tried to draw in air, desperate for it, needing oxygen like I hadn't a moment before. I choked on a thick layer of dust. My body had seized up, hands like rigid claws, spine rolled up in a fetal ball. My feet cramped, and my eyes were crusted closed. Everything felt hot and dry. I was encased in ash. It floated into my nose and throat, tasting of blood and bitter regrets. I had wanted Kaitlyn's blood. Adelle had turned me, starved me to the point of madness, and made me feed. I'd fed on Kaitlyn.

And I'd burned, but I'd survived. *Because I was human again.*

My memory flowed around patchy images of torture and madness.

It delivered me memories from what felt like so long ago. Kaitlyn, swimming in the pool of the house where I held her captive. Kaitlyn, eating, her tongue licking crumbs from one corner of her mouth. Kaitlyn's eyes crinkling, and her head tilting back to expose the slim arch of her neck—not for feeding on, but in laughter. Kaitlyn, looking wistfully at the waves, and telling me she'd never be happy unless she was free. Kaitlyn, staring into my eyes and telling me she was pregnant.

I broke away from the agony that imprisoned me, soaring on memories of her and me together, of the love and blood that made me human. Of the woman who'd made me whole and happy for the first time in my long and too-lonely life.

I dared to move, pushing free of the of ash around me, emerging from my chrysalis. I worried for a moment that when I stood up, I'd crumble into nothingness. But I didn't. My skin burned and tingled but was whole and unblemished. My body ached all over, yet my heart pounded in my chest, throbbing away with life, real life.

Thanks to Kaitlyn.

Kaitlyn.

I turned and saw her on the floor beside me, motionless and covered in blood. She'd saved me. Injected me with something? Or was it her blood that had changed me? Or both? Then she'd flipped a coin that had filled the room with sunlight. *Did that really happen?*

It had, and it was *devastating.* Marduk's relic? She must have found it.

And I'd almost killed her.

I tried to kick my brain into gear. I had to act fast if I was going to save her. Her lips had turned blue from blood loss, and her neck had been savaged. *By me.*

I choked that thought away. That was Adelle's doing. I couldn't, and wouldn't, be responsible for it. I was not that monster anymore and never would be again.

I scanned the area around us. Piles of ash on the floor were all that remained of Adelle and Dante. A few thralls stood stunned around the room, slowly coming back to themselves. I hoped they would come to their senses quickly and free themselves of this house of horrors.

Beside Kaitlyn, a glint of gold caught my eye. The coin she'd flipped.

I snatched it up, and then cradled her into my arms. She was clammy and still, her pulse slow and weak. I couldn't stay there any longer, not for the thralls or for anything. I had to get Kaitlyn to safety, wherever that was for us now.

I carried her out through the tunnels, squinting as sunlight came into view.

Parked right outside the entrance was a long black car. I tensed.

A solidly tinted window rolled down just a fraction, and I heard Bertha's voice.

"Quick, bring her in here."

I hesitated, but I had few other options. I had no clear plan in mind, but would do anything to save Kaitlyn, even go back to the Synedrion.

The door opened as I dashed toward it, then it quickly slammed once I was inside.

I laid Kaitlyn as gently as I could along the seat, leaning her against my body.

Bertha sat on the long seat facing ours. Ewan, the Synedrion's doctor for humans, was beside her.

"Had quite the adventure, I see?" She tapped her fingers on crossed arms.

"Are you going to help Kaitlyn?" I snarled.

"Of course," she said, and the doctor got to work. He hung a couple of IV bags up by the car's coat hangers and then hooked Kaitlyn up before seeing to the wound on her neck. I noticed another bite mark on her wrist, and wondered if it was from my fangs as well.

Everything had all happened so fast, and I had no idea what state things were at with the Synedrion, or where we now stood. I looked between Kaitlyn and Bertha, unsure. "How? Why?"

"Lance tipped me off. He was awfully cryptic about trying to warn me not to involve the rest of the Synedrion, and how I'd be sorry if I treated you two badly. He seemed conflicted about it, but it looks like he made the right decision."

Bertha pointed at the liquids running into Kaitlyn's veins. "Something Shirina cooked up, since Kaitlyn is so prone to blood loss. A special replenishment formula just for her. I thought it might come in handy."

I could only nod, confused, trying to catch up. "Where is Lance?" And more importantly, why hadn't he come for us himself?

"Gone, somewhere. He can come back, as we have no proof of him being directly involved in the kidnapping of Kaitlyn, theft from the lab, and destruction of parts of the Sun Shrine. It looks more like Joss was involved in all of that."

I raised both eyebrows. They had been busy, and there must have been more to the story. I hoped Kaitlyn could tell me soon, but she was still unconscious and deathly cold.

I rubbed her fingers, hoping to warm them with

mine. The doctor shooed me away, needing her hands to clip heart monitors onto, to slide cannulas in. I let him, and waited impatiently, a lump in my throat.

"You're human?" Bertha stared at my mouth, and I wiped at it, discovering it was wet with Kaitlyn's blood. I took an offered wet-wipe and cleaned myself up as best I could.

I quickly explained what Adelle and Dante had done, how they'd made me feed on Kaitlyn. I glossed over how Kaitlyn had managed to defeat them both, muttering something about stakes and being too out of it to see for sure what had happened as Kaitlyn's blood changed me.

Bertha tapped a few controls on the touch screen beside her, and the automated car began moving away. "I've already called in some Ebonguard to check the place over. To see what can be recovered. But for now, let's get you two home."

"That place isn't my home." Kaitlyn's voice was a raspy whisper, her eyes still closed and her body still.

I brushed my hand down her cheek, cleaning away drying blood and ash. "Shush," I chided, despite loving the sound of her voice, loving that she had awakened. "Rest."

"Can't rest. Need to kill Lance for snitching on us. Would have been a clean getaway," she grumbled.

"You can't even open your eyes," I replied, my smile growing.

"Can too." Her eyelids twitched, and her nose wrinkled, but her eyes didn't open. "Maybe later." Her forehead wrinkled. "I thought I'd killed you." She turned her cheek into my open palm. "You feel warm. The Remortalis worked."

Bertha's eyebrows both shot way up.

Kaitlyn gasped. "The … the *thing*. The THING. Owen, did you *get the thing*? We need the thing."

"The thing?"

She struggled, as though trying to get up from the seat and go back to where we came from. She whispered, "My lucky coin."

I squeezed her softly in my arms, made my voice soothing. "I got the thing."

She relaxed, right away. "Thank fuck. That thing is our ticket."

"Is she okay? She seems to be having a strange reaction to the medication," the doctor inquired, leaning across to take Kaitlyn's pulse.

"You're a strange reaction," she retorted. Her eyes finally opened, clear and green, looking up at me.

"I think she's fine. I think she's going to be more than fine." I kissed her on the forehead. My brave, resilient, amazing Kaitlyn.

"What about"—her voice caught, and her eyes turned glossy—"what about the pregnancy?"

"Have you had any bleeding? Abdominal discomfort?" the doctor asked.

"Only bleeding from the neck, which I know isn't the kind of bleeding you were being vague about, but it was a lot." She looked back at me. "Not your fault."

"I know."

The doctor shrugged. "Too early to say. We can keep you monitored and do some tests when we're in a better medical facility than the back of a car on a bumpy dirt road."

Kaitlyn nodded, then wrapped her hands around mine. I felt the brush of metal and saw a glint of diamond.

"You're wearing the ring. You found it," I said.

She held her right hand out, looking at it herself. "Yeah. I hope you don't mind."

"Well, actually ..." I delicately plucked the ring from her finger. "This is a family heirloom. I was supposed to give it to the woman I wanted to spend my entire life with, but then I waited centuries without finding a true love. I didn't think I'd ever use it."

"Oh." Her hands closed up, and drew away, but I took her left hand back into mine.

It was over. I knew it, and she did too. This nightmare was coming to a close. The cure had seemed to work, and they had no more reason to hold us prisoner. There was the chance Alam's hunters might come for us, or the Synedrion would want to dispose of us, but now we had our *ticket*. Kaitlyn had acquired for us something that no vampire would stand against. We were not going to be hidden away anymore, kept from our lives out of fear of anyone or anything. We were done living in twilight and darkness. We were done with vampires.

We were ready to move on with our lives. Free. Together.

We jostled against each other in the back of the car, and her drip tubes tangled between us. We were both covered in ash and blood and sweat and tears.

"Kaitlyn French, will you marry me?"

"Is this real?" Tears and laughter streamed from Kaitlyn. "Are you really asking me to marry you?"

"I am." I held the ring in front of her. She still leaned against me, almost in my lap, so I couldn't kneel. But I also couldn't wait a moment longer. "I have waited so many lifetimes to find a love like ours. You have made me human, and made me want to be a better person. You've saved my life and my heart over and over, and now they belong to you, entirely. I want to spend every moment of my existence with you. You are my future."

Kaitlyn's eyes fluttered closed, and for a moment I feared she'd fallen unconscious again. But a smile spread, brightening her whole face, and she looked up at me. "Ask me again."

"Will you marry me?"

"Yes!" she shouted.

I slid the ring onto her correct finger.

Bertha and Ewan clapped politely.

I bent down and placed a tender kiss onto Kaitlyn's lips. The kiss grounded me, filled me with a joy of life that felt like it could shine out of my skin. Even here, even now, in this terrible place, in the midst of so much awfulness, there was light and love and laughter, and I could feel all those things thanks to her. My heart swelled, fuller with every breath.

"Ouch," Kaitlyn mumbled between our lips.

I supported her head and lowered her into my lap, letting her rest.

She smiled, and that smile grew cheeky. "I do want to marry you, Owen. But ..."

"But?"

"The only way to stop people from thinking I was in rehab is to tell them the truth."

Bertha frowned. "You can't—"

"I'm going to have to tell them I fell in love with an incredible man and ran off to Europe to be with him. That means you can't hide anymore. You have to start going out with me in public."

My lips spread in a wide smile. "I'm looking forward to it."

Kaitlyn turned to address Bertha. "And I can do whatever I want now. I'm not going to be your prisoner anymore. I'm going to make my own rules. We will be walking away from this shadow world, the Synedrion, all of this." She turned back to me, smiled, then closed her eyes. "As soon as I can walk again. And no one will dare to stop us."

Epilogue

KAITLYN

The castle—*my* castle, I could still barely believe— was alive with the sounds of laughter and music. They flowed into the ballroom from out on the grounds where the guests were gathering, and my body swayed in time with the slow tempo playing. Flowers covered every surface, red roses and white wisteria emerging out of beds of wild strawberries, their lush green leaves spotted with ruby red fruit. Their fragrance filled in the air and I breathed the aroma in with a large smile on my face. Under that scent was just the faint hint of the perfume both Owen and I wore every day now; a custom blend on a base of unscented Nemexia essence.

Caterers were setting up the tables, decking them with white linens and fine china, antique silverware and delicate wine glasses. The floors, solid white marble, were gleaming and ready to be danced upon. I was meant to be doing final checks and getting ready, but I just stood there, taking in all the fairy tale gloriousness.

"Aren't you supposed to be dressed by now?"

The familiar voice swung me around. "Bertha? But it's, uh …"

I glanced from the huge windows through which bright daylight streamed in, back to her.

She chuckled. "Don't worry. I'm not going to blow up and ruin your nuptials. I took the cure. It's still in early stages. Lin and Shirina want to observe some of the first cured for a long period before it's widely available, but I talked them into letting me be part of their trial."

I snatched in a breath and looked her over. She seemed nearly the same as before, pale skin and pixie-cut, her teenage body in a perfectly fitted red gown suited to a femme fatale. And her eyes were green and brown? Heterochromatic, one of each color.

"Wow. You look amazing. Although, you're going to have to learn to dress your age. I suppose. Eh, screw it, what is age really, anyway?"

"Something I'm looking forward to experiencing, that's what." Her smile held a soft and wonderful emotion. "You have no idea how much it sucks to have people consider you immature just because your body stopped aging at sixteen.”

I barked a laugh. “I know people who would kill for that.”

“Yes, but would they be killed for it?”

“You’ve clearly not met the guests from Hollywood yet.”

She snorted. “It is good to see you again, Kaitlyn, and you look well.” Her gaze went to my belly. “You must be happy that it’s …”

She paused. I knew what she meant without her having to finish that sentence.

I was showing now, just a little. The baby was growing normally, and the relief over that was so sweet and pure that I often hugged that feeling to myself, glowing just to remember that this child was ours. Not mine and a vampire’s. Ours, mine and Owen’s. Two human beings having a nice, normal human baby.

“Very happy. Now, I know I didn’t send any invites to vampires for our wedding, you know, given the time of day.”

Bertha shrugged, and unabashedly picked a strawberry from one of my floral displays and popped it in her mouth. She made a face. “Oh, they are so tart!”

“The wild ones are,” I said. “Why are you here?”

She held something up for me to see. “I noticed this out on the gifts table. Thought I should bring it to your attention sooner rather than later.”

A black envelope with a silver stamp showing a blade surrounded by a ring of fire.

Dread flickered over me. "From the Blades of Alam?" There it was, proof they knew of us, and knew where to find us. But also proof they hadn't done anything with that knowledge, yet.

"Should I open it?" I asked.

"Well yes. That is why I brought it in for you."

"Is it safe?"

Bertha managed a perfect teenaged eye-roll. "I doubt it's going to explode poison all over you."

"For all we know, it might. If this ruins my wedding day, I am going to be very upset." I took the envelope gingerly and slit the side open with a finger. My eyes darted back and forth over the letter, and then a smile appeared.

"It's from ... an old friend!" *Joss! She's okay!*

It was a short message, details terse and minimal, in true Joss fashion.

"You have friends in the Blades?" Bertha asked with raised eyebrows.

I bit my lip at my slip up. "No, of course not. I was being sarcastic, you know? Like, oh, my old buddies that tossed me out an airplane that time!"

Yep, I was still relying heavily on my acting skills to keep me out of trouble. I looked over the letter again. Joss didn't explicitly say she was part of the Blades of Alam now, or whether she was still a vampire, or whether she was still blind. I swallowed my remaining guilt over that. I wondered whether Lance was still keeping her company.

"It's an invitation to us, Owen and me, letting us know that we would be welcome to join the Blades."

Bertha asked softly, as though without any judgement, "Would you be interested in that? Becoming an official vampire hunter?"

I cackled out a hard laugh. "No way! I don't want anything to do with any of that ever again."

She considered me for a moment and nodded. "Apart from coming across the letter, the reason I'm here today, is that now I'm cured, I've become a sort of human liaison to the Synedrion. For a while at least. I wanted to let you know that there are some new laws in place."

"We're not bound to vampire law," I pointed out, but Bertha continued.

"It has been made illegal to give a vampire the cure without their consent, by vampire or human. Luckily, the law came into effect after you did so to Owen—yes, we found the syringe—so we are letting that one slide. They're also forming new laws around the treatment of humans in general."

I smacked her hand away as she reached for another strawberry. "Smart, since some of you are becoming human."

I didn't bother mentioning that the ethical treatment

of animals hadn't exactly been a deterrent to humans when it came to food, and vampires are way more ruthless than even we are when hungry. "How will all this affect us? Me, Owen, our child?"

"You're all protected under our new laws. Any who follow Synedrion law will not harm you."

I nodded in a sharp, damn-straight kind of way. But that still left those who didn't follow Synedrion law. My spine straightened. So be it. I had the coin, and I had survived it all even before that. If anyone, or anything, came for me or Owen or our child, I was ready. We were free from vampire claims and rules. We could protect ourselves now and didn't need bodyguards anymore, no Ebonguard hiding in the shadows.

We'd only spent a single day with the Synedrion after dealing with Adelle and Dante. Just enough time for me to get the strength back to be able to walk away from there forever. After explaining the power of the coin, no one came after us, despite grumbles of us stealing a precious relic. I knew that Ri's flute and, much to the Synedrion's surprise, Tiamat's ring had been recovered from the lair. They believed Dante must have had it all along, and didn't connect it to Owen. Damkina's veil burnt up when Adelle did. At least that meant no more vampires returning from the dead.

"The lab is close to cracking artificial blood as well, it's already in trials too. Seems the pregnancy

was all that was needed to fulfill that prophecy after all," Bertha said.

"I hope so. I don't want anyone coming after my child," I replied. I had so many hopes for this child, and its future. Hope it would be healthy, and safe. But maybe I could only hope for those things as much as any parent could hope that for their child. Even the mundane world and life had risks and challenges. And I was ready to be there for it all.

"I don't think they'd dare." Bertha reached out and brushed a finger over the coin that I wore around my neck. Owen had it set into a circle of gold, one that allowed the coin to spin freely at a moment's notice, if it was needed. It wobbled, and Bertha stilled it under her fingertip.

I cleared my throat. "I actually do need to go and get dressed."

Bertha nodded, and took a few steps away. "I'll be in the audience, cheering you guys on."

I watched her go, watched her touching the flowers, smelling them, stealing another strawberry, and turning her face to the sunlight.

Then I went back to the dressing room set aside for me. It was quiet, and I stood there for a little while, just breathing.

Soon, everyone was there with me, my family and bridesmaids, helping me to dress. It was noisy and joyful, and I laughed and cried as the artist tried

to get my makeup done, scolding me happily as she re-did my eye-liner.

I was enveloped in hugs and giggles, and all the nightmares of the past fell away in the folds of antique lace and silk. Before I knew it, I was dressed and ready. My dark hair was pulled up high and piled onto the top of my head in curling tendrils bejeweled with silver leaves. The dress was long, flowing, with an Empire waistline to help hide my growing baby bump. It swished and swayed around me like the most delicate bell ever created, and I longed to dance in it. The veil, long and sheer, trailed down to my ankles and mingled its folds into those of my glorious dress.

I took a deep and very shaky breath. I'd never imagined myself married, not really. I'd been too busy imagining myself as an actor. I'd also never believed in true love until I fell in love with Owen. Tears misted my vision. It was so perfect, all of it. The stuff of dreams and fantasy, but real and mine.

A sweet, simple joy hit me hard, right in the chest. Joy that I could go be here, getting married to the man I loved, and that he could be present in my public life and not have to be a hidden figure just moving through the background of it all.

That was a true and immense pleasure. He didn't have to hide from vampires who would kill him for being cured, or me for creating the cure. With the first vampires already choosing to become human again, soon there would be many like Owen. The world had changed so much, so fast. I was still constantly scared for our child to be, but also in awe of all they would experience in their life. I supposed those feelings were a core part of becoming a parent.

I clutched at my trailing bouquet and then the door opened. I stepped out of the dressing room and into a short hallway with my eyes still watery, my breath coming hard and fast, and my heart ticking along at a happy and hectic pace.

The music started and I stepped down the aisle, where Owen was at the end waiting for me. The man I loved so very much. His hair was freshly barbered, and his dark suit and crisp white shirt and cuffs caught my eye. He was so handsome, so solid and real, and he stood in a long bar of sunlight that fell in through a window, haloing him. The glow outlined his every feature, and he took my breath away. I forgot all about the carefully rehearsed steps that were supposed to lead me to him in time to the music and broke into a run.

"I dooooo!" I hollered the words as I bolted down the aisle, and because I just couldn't stop myself, I hurled my body at his and kissed him deeply.

All the guests howled with laughter and applauded. The woman who was marrying us looked nonplussed as I broke away from Owen and our kiss. I grinned at her, totally unashamed of my antics.

Owen chuckled. "Um, maybe we should start the ceremony first?"

Laughter swelled all around us, and that was how we were married, in a long column of golden sunshine with laughter spilling from our mouths, with our hands joined and hearts entwined.

We were there, with so many of our dreams having come true, and still more to first dream up and then create. We were in love, happy, and healthy, and the sun would come up in the morning, and we would watch it shine its light down on us, together.

It was hard to believe anymore that he was once a vampire. That he once stole me and held me captive so he could feed from me. His Strawberry. That he was once a creature of the darkness, of dark feelings and dark actions.

Now, my every feeling was for them. For Owen and our unborn child. I would do anything to protect this love, these feelings, this family.

Because without them, my entire sunlit life would just go dark.

When we'd danced all we could dance, and ate all we could eat, and enjoyed as much of our guests' company as we could, I stole away up into the tower bedroom of the castle, *my* castle, with Owen, *my* Owen, for my perfect, fairy tale, happy ending.

The End

ABOUT THE AUTHOR

Lena Fox is a pen name of Selina Fenech. Professional daydreamer, Selina Fenech writes "adorably dark" Epic and Urban Fantasy for teens and adults. Filled with sweet and quirky characters, laugh out loud moments, and breath-taking adventures, her unique worlds are perfect for readers who love thrilling twists paired with happily ever afters.

Artist, mother, and cancer survivor, Selina is determined to live life to the fullest, and loves escape rooms, gardening, and all forms of food and geekery.

Selina also applies her distinctive take on magical realms as a world-renown fantasy artist and has published many illustrated books, oracle decks, and colouring books.

FIND OUT MORE
ABOUT SELINA

Official Website www.selinafenech.com

NEED MORE TO READ?

Discover more urban fantasy, paranormal romance, contemporary romance, young adult, epic fantasy, fairy tale retellings and more from Lena Fox and Selina Fenech.

Visit www.selinafenech.com
to sign up for a free sampler library!